DANIEL WEISBECK

STATUS HUMAN

BOOK TWO OF

THE UPSILON SERIES

Publisher, Copyright, and Additional Information

Status Human by Daniel Weisbeck, published by DJW Books

www.danielweisbeckbooks.com

Copyright © 2022 by Daniel Weisbeck

PART 1

_ONLY HUMAN
AFTER ALL

ONE

UPSILON ANDROIDS WERE NOT DESIGNED for fishing. Not as a pre-installed start-up application anyway. An upgrade would have been handy as I struggled to hold on to the bluefin writhing in my hands. Kirstjen tried to hide his laughter. His father, Gunnar, with his silver beard, deeply weathered skin, and chalky white complexion, grunted discouragingly and shook his head. Gunnar's disappointment was justified. I may be stronger than a human. I may have rapid reflexes and can analyze a situation at near-light speeds. But I was proving useless for sorting through their morning catch. I let the dying bluefin squirt back into the waves rocking our boat, which elicited another grunt and an additional explanative eye roll from Gunnar.

"Get those fish into the box and be quick about it, Kirst," he grumbled at his son while staring unwelcomingly at me with side eyes. "Then let the net out," he continued. "We have time for one more round."

I didn't need my quantum computer to figure out Gunnar was not pleased I had joined their morning trawl. Fishing was their family's livelihood and Kirstjen, his only son, was his lone helper. They couldn't afford any distractions, especially not an inexperienced young girl his son had just met. And if Gunner got this upset over a simple girl coming aboard their boat, imagine his reaction had he known his son's new girlfriend wasn't even human. That's right. Kirstjen and his father had no idea I was an android.

I didn't want to lie to Kirstjen about my identity. Our relationship should never have happened. I was instructed not to talk to anyone on the island outside of absolute necessity. And even then, I was never to reveal who I was or what I was. But a human life rarely goes as planned, even for an android.

I started my existence as a highly advanced bio-robotic android booted up with the Host Neural Code (HNC) of a twelve-year-old human named Jenna Finster. I was designed to be a replicant of the deceased child for her father, Ben Finster. (He was an evil man whose life came to a tragic and justified end. I made sure of that.) I would have spent my life locked away in his cellar if not for Professor Bobby Houndstooth (Teacher), head of Anthropomorphism Programming at Nomad Robotics, who, during a service visit to Finster's house to understand why I was malfunctioning, realized I had somehow become a sentient life form. Instead of terminating me, she helped me escape. Together we learned that a rouge ex-Nomad scientist named Charlie had given me a gene-editing virus that mutated in my wetware drive brain, gifting me self-awareness. Things sort of went crazy for us after that. The kind of crazy where Charlie and many other people ended up dead. That was how Teacher and I had come to this island, living undercover, on the run from some seriously nasty people, like Nomad Robotics, the world-leading robotics corporation secretly building an army of soldier androids. One of which had run away—that would be me. So yeah, there were a few good reasons I had to lie to Kirstjen about my identity.

Kirstjen worked at his father's fish stall on the island's main harbor docks. Their stand was part of an old outdoor market: a long series of pitched tarps and wood shacks where fishermen, farmers, and craftspeople sold their wares to the villagers from seven in the morning to noon five days a week. It was the sort of place you smelt long before you saw it. The briny scent of sea animals mixed with pungent cheeses and freshly baked pastries. (I've analyzed and logged the chemical makeup of that scent in my database should I want to recreate it for nostalgic reasons.) The old market was a near-perfect representation of the photographs from the early 1800s posted on the visitor's board outside its entrance. The open network of stalls was part of the town's history and was legally protected. The entire little port village, with its picture-perfect wood-clad buildings painted in bright yellow, red, and blue, nestled into the rugged coastline around an ancient stone harbor, was a world heritage Non-Invasive Technology Zone. Low-tech, off-the-grid, old school was not just a way of life on the island; it was like a religion. The very reason it was such a good hiding place for an android. And why this android had to pretend to be human.

The market was about as safe as it would get for me to mix with the villagers. The crowded narrow passages and makeshift stalls stacked one next to the other created a loud, congested, busy scene of daily shoppers, so it was easy for me to blend in. And that the market closed at noon gave it a sense of constant urgency. Stall owners and shoppers didn't have time for idle chit-chat. Again, perfect for someone trying to avoid conversations.

Traveling to the market became a daily chore I had invented for myself while Teacher holed herself up in the cellar of our tiny cottage on the outskirts of town. Down there, she had built a makeshift lab where she spent her days trying to unravel the miracle of the genetic mutations in my organic brain. Going to the market was a chance for me to get out on my own and exercise being alive. Living was something new for me, and I needed a lot of practice at it—a lot. Jenna's memories were still etched into my brain, but that was only a past. I was trying to build a future.

When I first saw Kirstjen, I had planned to make a fish stew. (Cooking was one of my human hobbies I had learned while on the island. It turns out I'm a great chef—if I have a recipe to follow. I have added this skill to the list of human things I'm good at —fighting, killing, lying, and now cooking. Things are moving in the right direction.) My usual pattern was to shop the stalls at the edges of the market if I needed a quick exit. But on this day, I was reluctantly drawn into the market center looking for the right ingredients. Scanning the stalls, I chose the most crowded fish stand I could find and slipped into the queue without raising any attention. We were a line-up of at least six people. I kept my eyes to the ground to avoid contact with others in line. To distract myself, I repeated my order in my head: *Cuttlefish, cuttlefish, cuttlefish.*

The line moved steadily, but with each person served, at least one or more arrived behind me. I could feel their eyes pushing in on my back and gazing over my shoulder, silently urging everyone ahead to hurry up. It had been a long time since I had been in such a confined space with so many people. I twisted my fingers into pretzel knots. It was a Jenna nervous habit written into my code. Hard to break.

When the woman in front of me placed her order at the fish counter, I glanced up. The boy working behind the stand, whom I hadn't noticed before, had his back to us. He seemed young, about my age. His flaxen hair was thick and wavy and hung down like a mop on his head below his ears. I hadn't given him much consideration. I was busy preparing for a quick exit. Just when I was feeling good about getting out of the market without incident, the boy behind the counter turned around. That was when my life, or the life I was trying to create, changed forever. A rogue current surged through my body. I think Jenna would call it a crush. Whatever it was, it sent my clock speeds racing and my internal temperature rising. He had ocean blue eyes, illuminated as if backlit. His broad, hypnotizing smile squeezed the current out of my heart-box battery. System alerts rang through my network like a chorus of church bells, and my knees felt weak. (A metaphoric simulated response, of course, as my knees were graphene reinforced hydraulic hinges.) A wave of biochemical signals rushed out of my wetware drive brain and disabled my quantum processor's hyperthreading capabilities, leaving me with a single-thread focus on nothing but the boy behind the counter.

The woman in front of me accepted her package, transferred her credits to his scanner and moved out of line, leaving me face-to-face with 'Kirstjen,' as spelled out by his name stitched onto the chest of his white coat.

Confused by my system malfunctions and dumbstruck to speechlessness, I had forgotten what I was about to order. And if my silence wasn't embarrassing enough, I couldn't stop staring at him. I knew I was holding his gaze for far too long without speaking. Things got very awkward quickly. Someone behind me cleared their throat impatiently.

"How can I help you?" Kirstjen asked me.

His voice was young but deep. I imagined it would become huskier later in his life after the human growth phase completed its cycle. I guessed him to be around sixteen years old.

He waited patiently for my response. When he noticed I was struggling, he smiled and said: "How about the sea bream? It's one of my favorites."

My body was designed to replicate human emotional responses, which would explain why my cheeks were burning red in response to his voice. A feature I would have liked kept hidden at that moment.

"Okay. I'll take two," I said abruptly and smiled shyly. (So much for the cuttlefish recipe.)

My limited experience with flirting (zero experience) left me feeling like I was doing everything wrong. Jenna's memories were proving to be little help. She died long before she had a chance to flirt with boys, much less master it.

To make things worse, he suddenly broke eye contact. It was expected, as he had to turn around and prepare my fish. But somehow, it felt like a personal betrayal and triggered a whole other series of very annoying emotional responses in me like insecurity, fear, and self-doubt. I don't know how humans ever started a relationship when the data coming from the opposite party was so inconclusive and conflicting. And all of this happened in less than five minutes!

Desperate to know if he felt the same attraction, I resorted to my best asset, quantum analysis. I replayed our conversation and reviewed the facts. There was a slight speeding up of his heart rate according to my medical scanner; his cheeks flushed pink when I spoke; and he held direct eye contact for a considerable time. His voice's tenor was pleasant and inviting. There was a lean into the counter, getting closer to me, when he suggested sea bream. Considering everything, I thought the odds he liked me in return were good, but the algorithm I spun up only gave me a sixty-five percent chance he shared my spontaneous crush or, at the least, was interested in me, no matter how many times I recalculated. And I recalculated many times while he had his back to me.

Whatever it was between us, it nearly ended when he handed me my sea bream, took payment in credits, and called on the next person in the queue. I knew I had to move out of the line, but I couldn't. The contents of my recycler started spinning. Air stuck in my lung-box oxygenator like a held breath at the thought of never talking to him again. I waited stupidly, holding my dead fish in a bag, until, in sympathy, he tilted his head, beamed a smile that cut straight through me, and said, "Let me know how you like it."

"Maybe," I giggled.

Kirstjen pinched his face and snapped his

head back as if I was speaking a foreign language. He was right. Maybe? And giggling? Oh, God. What kind of response was that? It was one of a hundred possible responses provided by the algorithm I had spun up to help me with my flirting. Clearly, I had picked the wrong one, but it was too late to correct the error. Humiliated, I turned away and quickly disappeared into the crowd, running out of the market in embarrassment, self-loathing, and weirdly an elevated joy that felt like floating. How can all these feelings exist together?

That evening, Teacher enjoyed a steamed sea bream and samphire dinner. I struggled to enjoy anything. I couldn't stop thinking about Kirstjen's smile and my ridiculous "Maybe". A silly game Jenna had played with a flower kept repeating in my head while we ate: He loves me. He loves me not. The memory was blurry, so I might have made it up. I wasn't thinking straight. Luckily, Teacher was too busy talking about her research to notice I wasn't listening.

Later that night, I was in my bed staring out my window at a crescent moon in the sky, unable to shut down for a night of sleep. By midnight, I had spun through a thousand scenarios where Kirstjen and I had fallen in love and lived happily together. Sometimes it started slowly, without him knowing he was falling in love with me. Other times it was instant passion and devotion to each other until the end. In one case, we even had children together. Seriously, Jenna's imagination was out of control. But one major obstacle never entered our little love stories. I wasn't human; therefore, he would never love me.

My battery was low, not critical, but I was done pretending I could live a happy human life anyway, so I forced a hard shut down. It was the only way I would be able to turn off for the night. I set a timer for a reboot at five AM. Nice and early when the market opened. Yes. I was going back for more humiliation. I couldn't help myself.

The following day, Teacher was up in the kitchen waiting for me. That wasn't unusual. She was the kind of person who thought sleep was for the weak. *"Work to be done in the lab,"* she would say. *"Your brain isn't going to figure itself out."* Which is odd to say because my organic brain and my Kernel, the quantum computer that sat between the bottom of my wetware drive brain and the top of my cabled spinal cord, were superior to a human's ability to process data. So technically, my brain should have figured itself out. However, it turns out that analysis of data, no matter how much there is or how fast you can get through it, is not the same as conjuring a hypothesis. Humans can innately use their life experiences to inspire ideas that seem to come out of thin air. Because Jenna, my human, was so young when she died and had zero experience with bioengineering, Teacher had a solid lead on me for theorizing on my gene mutations, both what had happened and where it might lead to in my evolution. I left her to it. I had more important things to understand like cooking, combat training, and falling in love—the important stuff.

"What are your plans for today?" Teacher asked.

"I'm heading to the market early. I've got a new fish recipe I want to try out tonight."

"Fish again, eh? I'm starting to think you are becoming a carnivore," she laughed at her own joke. "You know, nobody but these villagers, hunt animals anymore. Meat comes from biomass generators, where it should. If you ask me, it's creepy how they go out every day to kill something."

"I was designed to kill things. Human things. Do you find me creepy?"

"Depends on the day," she chuckled again.

I had learned Teacher's humor over our last few months together. It was often sarcastic and not that funny. But Teacher insulted the people she liked and trusted. I trusted her as well. However, not enough to tell her the truth. She would have been furious at me if she knew my intentions were to strike up a conversation with Kirstjen, a human villager who could expose our hiding place and get us both killed. But one thing Jenna had taught me about being human is that sometimes following an instinct, even when it goes against all the odds streaming through my statistical algorithms, can lead to necessary lessons and growth. Humans make bad decisions all the time. They called it taking risks. So, if I wanted to learn who I really was as an individual,

I needed to take more risks. Even if those choices turned out to be mistaken. (And don't ask me the statistical odds that chasing Kirstjen was a mistake. I ignored that.)

When I arrived, the market was buzzing with shoppers, having just opened for business. Seeing the crowds offered me some comfort, but not enough to unwind the knot of anxiety that had built up on the walk down the hill from our cottage. I was so preoccupied with planning what to say I couldn't remember the journey to the market. Luckily, I have an AI autopilot program on my Kernel.

I hesitated outside the market's main entrance, rehearsing my options one last time.

"Oh, Kirstjen, your suggestion of sea bream was amazing. You really know your fish." Nope, that was way too cheesy.

"Hi, Kirstjen." (Attempt a shy giggle.) *Since you asked...the sea bream was amazing, I thought I would come back for more."* Sea bream two days in a row? Nope, too obvious.

Who was I kidding? No matter what I said, all I could hear in the back of my mind was, *"Hello, Kirstjen. It's me, the girl who is not an android, from yesterday. That's right, I'm human. I promise."*

Compelled by a mysterious force beyond the logic of algorithms and statistical odds, I took a leap of faith and winged it. What could go wrong? Everything, that is what the data was telling me. Everything could go terribly wrong. I carried on anyway.

Ushered by the familiar chorus of stall owners advertising their products, villagers placing orders, and bleating seagulls pacing on the outskirts of the market's boundary, I made my way to the center of the market quickly. When I arrived at the location of Kirstjen's fish stall, I looked up and froze in utter horror. He wasn't there. Gunnar, his father, was behind the counter taking orders. The market's sounds, colors, and smells started spinning around me. I was suddenly suffocating in a sea of enemies. All eyes were on me, the faker, the robot among them. I had willingly and stupidly exposed myself. And for what?

In a panic, I turned, ready to run out of the market and all the way home. Before my feet could move, I was blocked. Something like a squeak escaped from my mouth. Standing in front of me, having come up from behind my back, was Kirstjen. I nearly punched him in the larynx in surprise. I made a note to remind him to never sneak up on a killer robot.

"Sorry, I didn't mean to frighten you," he said.

Do humans hear trumpets when they fall in love? I swear I heard trumpets when he spoke. To be specific, *Trumpet Sonata No. 1 in F Major: I. Allegretto.*

"Um, no—You didn't." I stuttered, smiled, and blushed, following my internal instructions on feminine coyness.

I heard Kirstjen's heart beat faster and his

pupils dilated. *Lessons on Feminine Coyness* were working. Good to know.

"How was the sea bream?" he asked.

"The sea bream was amazing," I answered eagerly. "You really know your fish." (Yep, it sounded as stupid out loud as it did in my head.)

Kirstjen burst into laughter. "You are kind of odd," he said.

Warning alarms rang through my network. I sensed he meant his words warmly. But I was odd, like android kind of odd. The conversation on my lack of social skills was too risky a thread to follow. I needed to calm down and behave like a normal person.

"Sorry, I'm nervous."

"Are you visiting the island? I haven't seen you before."

"Sort of." Keeping my answers short and nonspecific gave the best odds of avoiding exposure as a liar.

"Well, then, allow me to officially welcome you to our island," he said, extending his hand. "I'm Kirstjen."

I almost said, *"I know your name. I've repeated it over the last twelve hours at least a thousand times."*

"I'm Silon."

We shook hands. Kirstjen's grip was firm, his palm calloused. I kept the contact between our hands short and my squeeze light just in case he sensed something was off with my body. But our eyes remained locked in a beautiful infinite moment of silence. Which quickly became more awkward than romantic.

"Were you coming back for more…fish?" He blushed deep red.

"Yes, if you have another recommendation?"

That morning I left with two paper-wrapped cod fillets, hand-carved by Kirstjen himself, to the annoyance of the other customers waiting in line before me. I took that as a sign that Kirstjen wanted to see me again. And I returned faithfully every morning in the days that followed. (Teacher ate a lot of fish that week.)

With each visit, our conversations lasted a little longer. I stood on the sidelines of his fish stall while he talked about the catch of the day, his father, and their boat. I mostly listened. Gunnar grumbled as he took over serving the customers.

Our smiles gave way to shy giggles, eventually trust, and then compliments of an obvious flirting nature. I hardly recognized myself. But to be honest, that is how I spent most of my days—feeling unrecognizable So, without much, if any, caution, I allowed him to believe I was human and allowed myself the experience of these new, overwhelming, and dangerously intense feelings.

TWO

On my seventh visit to Kirstjen's stall, he asked me to return later in the morning when the market was about to close. I knew it was a bad idea, but I couldn't help myself. I didn't dare go back to the cottage and risk running into Teacher only to come up with another lie about why I needed to go to the market twice in one day. So, I spent the next few hours hiding under the docks, deep in the shadows where I wouldn't be seen or spoken to. Counting the squawking birds hunting along the beach for discarded scraps kept my mind preoccupied while I waited. Time stretched out unbearably. At eleven forty-nine, I headed back up to the market. Things were quieting down. Shoppers were leaving rather than entering the market, and some stalls had packed up. I had never been to the market this late in the day. The empty lanes that crisscrossed through the old trading site felt foreign. As if I were in the wrong place. Being suddenly lost heightened the reoc-curring alarms in my head I hadn't been able to shut off since meeting Kirstjen. But I was getting good at ignoring my risk analysis auto alerts.

Kirstjen was loading boxes of left-over seafood into a cart with wheels when I approached. The rest of the world would have used levitating gliders to move heavy objects around. But not on Kirstjen's island. Although, after several conver-sations with him, I suspected that the island's young people were not as keen to shut out the world of technology and modern advances as their elders. I especially hoped it was true in Kirstjen's case.

Kirstjen smiled when he saw me. We were comfortable enough in each other's company at this point to skip the awkward blushes and stum-bling hellos. I rode with him as he drove his cart to his father's boat and told me funny stories about the customers who had visited him. Like Old Man Georg, who refused false teeth and pronounced the word salmon as "Thelma." Or Mrs. Lynna, who loved the taste of fish but hated the smell so much she had to pinch her noise while placing her order and sounded like she had swallowed a balloon full of helium.

At the boat, we threw the left-over fish over the side and into the water to the excitement of screeching birds waiting patiently for the daily ritual. Kirstjen's father, Gunnar, stayed back at the stand to clean up, so we had the afternoon to ourselves.

Kirstjen sensed I was uncomfortable in crowds and suggested we walk to a small private beach in an alcove nearby where we could be alone. It was the best day of my life. I've tagged those memories and created a hard drive copy to ensure I will never forget our first day alone together.

Kirstjen did most of the talking. That was intentional on my part. I had to keep the conversation focused on him as much as possible to avoid uncomfortable questions about me. My lies were becoming heavily weaved into reality and keeping them separate enough to hide my identity required significant multi-tasking from my processors.

As we sat on the beach, I listened to stories about his childhood growing up on the island. The afternoon sun warmed his golden face and peach-colored lips so he appeared as natural in the landscape as the bleached sands and azure ocean. Eventually, as the low sun on the horizon glowed red in the late afternoon hours, Kirstjen grew tired of talking about himself, and soon the questions came. I knew I had to share more about myself or risk ending the day. I couldn't let that happen.

I spun up a program on my Kernel designed to create a cover story if I was captured by an enemy. Within seconds I had a whole new back story. In this version of me, Teacher (whom I called Mother for Kirstjen's sake) and I were from New Zealand. She was a volcanologist, and we were visiting the island for her research. I also told him that my mother was shy. My strategy analyzer gave this story a near ninety-eight percent probability of being believable. The part about my mother being a recluse I added right at the end to head off what I estimated would be his next set of questions about why she never came into the village. And I didn't want him asking to come up to our tiny fishermen's cottage to meet her.

As I talked, Teacher's voice rang through my head. *"Do not engage with the locals other than for business. Do not linger. Do not talk about yourself or about why we are here. Even the tiniest detail could lead to being discovered by Nomad."*

I knew she was right. All best played-out strategies for our survival required anonymity. But survival had taken on a new meaning for me. Kirstjen had changed how I saw the world and what I wanted from it. It had only been a few weeks since I had known him, but it felt like we had been friends forever.

Over the next few days, we continued to sneak away together at the close of the market. We would sit alone under the docks with only the seagulls as company or explore the many small coves that lined the coastal village. Kirstjen was so good at finding places where we could be alone that the island felt like our own private paradise.

My story about being the daughter of a traveling scientist seemed to go down without suspicion. Kirstjen was far more preoccupied with how well I could speak his language. Of course, I didn't tell him I was programmed to speak over one hundred languages and five hundred dialects. So, I told him I always learned the languages of the places where my mother was working. It was my way of coping with moving around.

Lying was easier than I thought once I got started, thanks to my character development algorithm. Each new detail was carefully stored in a file, so I wouldn't forget the elaborate life I was creating. In this made-up world, anything was possible, and I could be anyone. The only problem was that I knew it was all make-believe, not just the stories but my relationship with Kirstjen. If he knew the truth about my identity, our relationship would end—badly. So, I told myself I had to be greedy. Get as much out of our relationship as I could before...before...what? That was the real problem. I didn't have an end game.

While tossing pebbles into the ocean waves on a black sand beach, Kirstjen went quiet one day. I could tell something was on his mind. After a long silence, he finally spoke.

"School will be starting in a week. Will you be joining our class?"

The aperture in my optical implants contracted tightly. It was the first time Kirstjen had brought up the future. Our future. A future together I knew was impossible but refused to think about—until now. As I spun up my character generation app and extrapolated a reasonable response, my torsion systems involuntarily tightened, and my recycler bubbled. The thought of disappointing Kirstjen left me nauseous and terrified.

"I don't think so," I said in a barely audible voice. "I already attend virtual school in my home country."

Kirstjen's expression broke. His jaw tensed and his gaze went to the sand. "But what if you visited our class as a guest," his voice went high and hopeful. "It could be interesting to learn more about where you are from."

"Maybe," I lied. "I would have to ask my mother, but she is strict about my school attendance. So it is easier for me when we go back home."

Kirstjen shifted his feet through the black sand anxiously. The conversation was not going as he had hoped. Between having to help his father on their fishing boat in the mornings and returning to school, he was becoming desperate to find a way for us to continue seeing each other. I had already thought about Kirstjen going back to school and how it would be a convenient opportunity for a natural break in our relationship before things got more complicated. But hearing the plea in his voice and sharing the same desire to be together at any cost put my AI logic and organic brain into direct conflict. That I might not see him again squeezed my heart-box. Being with Kirstjen made me want to break all the rules, even risk the horrible thought of getting caught.

"Maybe you could join me on my fishing boat?

Only if you want to," Kirstjen said, unwilling to give up on me.

I wanted to. I really, really wanted to. But this would require spending more time with his father, who, over the last few days with disagreeable grunts and hard stares, had made it clear he didn't approve of me and, worse, revealing to Teacher what I had been up to over the last few weeks. The odds of either going well were not in my favor. And yet...

"Okay," I said, ignoring the warning flashes from my network.

Kirstjen leaned into me, closing his eyes. I wasn't quite sure what to do. I knew he was about to kiss me, and I knew how to kiss—pucker my lips and lean in—but I had a sudden panic attack he might sense something was off with me if I let him get that close. I was led to believe that I feel and smell like a human to other humans, but I had never tested that theory so intimately. I couldn't move. Kirstjen stopped before reaching my mouth and opened his eyes to find a look of abject terror on my face.

"I'm sorry," his cheeks went red. Pulling back, his face contorted, shifted from embarrassment to confusion to frustration. "I thought you liked me like I like you," he said.

My heart-box sunk.

I leaned in quickly, kissing him on his slightly parted lips, and then pulled away before he could respond. Jumping up, I said, "Tomorrow morning then. I'll be at the docks before you head out."

I ran away. The warmth of his lips pressed against mine haunted me. *Did he feel the same?* I stole one last look back over my shoulder. He was standing up, hands in his pockets, chest held high, rocking on his heels like he was listening to a song in his head, and smiling from ear to ear. He did feel the same.

As I reached the edge of the village and started my way up the cliffside path to our small home, my ecstasy turned to dread. What was I going to tell Teacher? There was little in the village open at four AM, and even if there was, my need to go into town that early was unexplainable.

After a long, hard think and nearly two-thirds of the way home, I decided it was time to tell Teacher the truth about Kirstjen. She couldn't stop me from seeing him after all. I wasn't a real teenager. And she wasn't my real mother, even if she acted like it. Even so, she would be upset, and I didn't want to scare her. She risked her life to get me out of Finster's house and help me run away. And I know she thought of me as more than a science project. We were family. A kind of messed-up killer family on the run. But still family. She deserved to know I was in love—or I thought I was.

Back home, I made 'cheesies' and chips in honor of our lost friends Charlie and his android Nutt, my first friend. Melted cheese sandwiches were Nutt's favorite. I thought the sentiment might get her into the right mood.

Teacher arrived for dinner from her lab downstairs, looking tired. Her sunken eyes and uncombed hair pulled back into a quick knot reminded me how hard she had been working to help me. And how selfish I had been running around behind her back with no thought of the risk it brought for both of us. We were supposed to be looking out for each other.

"Cheesies? Have you been thinking about Nutt again?" she asked.

Grabbing the bottle of red wine I opened for her, she poured her glass nearly full and plopped down into her usual seat at our small, round dining table. I placed both plates on the table and joined her in my seat. Instantly, my knee bounced nervously under the table. (Another terrible habit Jenna had that I couldn't shake.)

"At least it's not more fish," Teacher joked, taking a long sip of wine before raising her glass.

I raised my glass of water in return.

"To Charlie and Nutt," Teacher stated. "The crazy motherfucker who invented sentient AI and his crazier android protégé, Nutt, who gave their lives to save ours."

I nearly cried when she mentioned Nutt's sacrifice back in the city. He died freeing me from my genetically coded tracking device by chasing our kidnapper's AI into their mainframe and setting their hard drives on fire, destroying all their data on me. Missing him only made me want to be with Kirstjen all the more.

I decided to wait until Teacher's wine glass

was half empty before telling her about Kirstjen. That didn't take long.

"Teacher," I interrupted as she bit into the melted cheese sandwich. I was hoping a mouthful of food would slow her response. "We've been on this island for three months, and I've noticed some villagers are starting to look at me funny. I imagine they are wondering who we are, what we are doing here, and how long we will stay."

"What do you mean?" her voice was high, worried, even with a mouth full of food. "Has someone been asking you questions?"

"Not yet." Okay, that was a lie. But for the right reasons. I needed to soften the blow of the truth. "However, I thought it might be better if we reach out first. Maybe make a few acquaintances and seed a cover story. Get ahead of any potential gossip that might encourage them to do more research on us."

I was feeling proud of the argument forming. Even I started to believe my excuse for breaking the rules. Spreading a cover story was a good idea. However, judging by the suspicion on Teacher's face, she disagreed. She stared at me hard and long in silence before taking another long drink of wine.

"You think we should start talking to the villagers...or you have done?" Her words were sharp and drawn out.

Crap. Human intuition sucks sometimes.

"I've only talked to one person. A boy from the fish market," I said nervously.

"What the fuck, Silon!" Her free hand slapped the table.

"Let me explain," I begged.

She didn't wait. Jumping up from the table with the wine glass in hand, she paced and drank rapidly.

"Shit—shit, shit, shit."

When Teacher got angry or nervous, she would swear. The more upset she was, the more she swore. This was a lot of swearing. I babbled on, hoping to calm her down.

"If I hadn't talked to Kirstjen, someone would have come knocking on our door asking questions. You know I am right."

Did she? Was I? There was a twenty percent chance I was wrong. I decided not to share that quantum computer-inspired statistic with her.

Teacher spun around and locked her eyes on mine. "Kirstjen? You're on a first-name basis with this person?"

"He's a nice person and would never do anything to hurt me."

Her eyes narrowed further and her stare grew harder if that was possible. "Do you have feelings for this…Kirstjen?"

My red cheeks could not lie. "Maybe."

My answer elicited an eye roll and a long sigh.

"What exactly did you tell him about us?"

Finally, we were getting somewhere. "You are a vulcanologist studying the island's dormant volcanoes. We are from New Zealand and I…I'm your daughter."

Teacher's face went blank, washed of rage. I wanted to believe sentimentality had broken her resistance. Calling her 'Mother' should have made her happy. This strategy had great odds of succeeding. But I soon realized her expressionless face was not a sign of unconditional love but calculation.

"I want to know who this kid is, where you met, and who else you talked to." Her questions were rapid-fire.

"He is sixteen and the son of a local fisherman named Gunnar. They have a fish stall in the old market where I met him. I've only talked to Kirstjen, no one else. And no, he doesn't know I am an android."

"That explains the fish dinners then!" Her hands went up into the air, causing the wine to spill on the floor. "And when he does figure out you are not human, because he will, what will you do then?"

Ouch. That hurt. Hearing Teacher say I was not human felt like a punch to the recycler. Maybe I wasn't born human, but I thought it would be her if anyone who would believe I could become one. I fought the tears welling up in my eyes. Nothing about this conversation with Teacher was going as planned.

"I won't let it get that far," I conceded.

"It's already too far, Silon. I don't understand why you are telling me this now, after weeks of lying."

"He asked me to join him on their next fishing trawl with his father. I want to go."

"No," her voice turned to a plea. "Please, for both our sakes, you need to end this."

Tears slipped down my cheeks. Stupid HNC emotions.

"I want to know what it is like. Having a boyfriend. Even if it has to end," I said.

Teacher paused as I wiped the tears from my face. Her brows arched sympathetically. Placing her wine glass down on the table, she knelt by my side and put her hands on my arm. "I want that for you as well, Silon. Really, I do. Hell, I want it for both of us. Not the male version, of course," she joked. "But this is not the time."

"When then," I snapped. I wasn't sure where the sudden burst of anger had come from. I knew Teacher was right. Yet something inside me came pouring out. "We have no idea how long we are supposed to stay on this island. Or if Leroy is coming back for us at all. We could grow old and die here. Or you could anyway. And then I will be left alone."

"I won't let that happen. I promise. We will go public as soon as I can replicate Charlie's gene mutations in your wetware drive. Nobody, not even Nomad or any government, will be able to stop that story."

"Let's go public now. I'm proof. And Leroy, he's like me."

"Without the ability to replicate the mutations, you are just a one-off phenomenon. A malfunction. That is how Nomad will label you. And you will be handed over to the government to be studied and torn apart. The science and the proof are the leverage, not you. And Leroy is just a ghost right now. We don't even know how to contact him. Nobody will believe he even exists."

Her reasoning had a near one hundred percent correct rating. Allowing Teacher time to unravel my brain was the most likely reason Leroy sent us to this tiny island to live in a fisherman's cottage with a hidden science lab underground, not so I could play human and fall in love. Damn Leroy. This was all his fault.

Weighing all the options and outcomes, which I did at lightning speeds, I knew she was right. "Okay, I promise to stop seeing him," I said.

Teacher's face relaxed. She stood and picked up her glass. Walking into the open plan kitchen and leaning back against the counter, she took a long swig of wine. "Well, I suppose I will have to learn a little bit about volcanoes now," she teased, trying to lighten the moment.

I had nothing to say anymore. I wanted to go to my room.

"Silon, I know it hurts, but it really is better. Not just for us but for his safety as well. That poor kid doesn't need to get wrapped up in all this shit."

"I know."

Teacher watched me sulk. After several minutes, a familiar, sly grin lit up her face. This is why I loved Teacher. No matter how bad things got or how badly I behaved, like doing things behind her back or, worse, killing people, she never stayed angry at me for too long. That smile meant she had given in, even if just a little.

"Maybe it *would be* best to let him down gradually, to avoid suspicion," she winked. "Go on the fishing trip. But afterwards, you must break up and stop seeing him. If you need some advice, I can give you tons of help on how to push people you care about away. My dating track record is a master class in avoidance."

This was her attempt at self-deprecating humor. But it was probably true. She was too obsessed with her work to give anyone a permanent role in her life. I was different. I was the object she was studying. I was her perfect companion, both android and human. And I knew how to make Teacher happy. Life was way more manageable if you let Teacher believe she was making all the decisions. Humans like to feel they are essential and necessary. For Teacher, that meant constantly feeling like my teacher.

"Yes, I could use your help," I said. Even though I didn't.

Teacher filled her near-empty glass of wine to the top and paced. "Okay. Let's role play. I'll be Kirstjen…"

Oh, God…

THREE

OUTSIDE, on the docks, it was dark and cold. Gunnar and Kirstjen were preparing their boat for the morning's fishing expedition. Their movements had a strong sense of habit, a set rhythm they had built over many fishing trips and many years. The sky was filled with stars. Three seagulls cried over our heads, anticipating the scraps soon following. I stood quietly on the docks near the boat, watching Kirstjen, my arms wrapped tightly around my body. The weather was not something I needed to worry about. But a young human girl would have found the biting sea air penetrating. I mentioned how cold it was several times and shivered occasionally. My replicator systems also altered the color of my flesh, particularly my lips, giving them a blueish hue.

"Hurry now, Kirst. We are already behind schedule," Gunnar ordered.

I had witnessed Gunnar talking at his son in a

similar tone back in the market: blunt and demanding. But I could tell, regardless of his faults, that Kirstjen loved his father. I could see it in his eyes. It hurt him when Gunnar barked orders and never said a nice thing. Even so, Kirstjen wanted to please his father. I hadn't experienced this behavior before—loving someone so much you would let them hurt you. It was all confusing for me. I could never have loved my father after what he did to me, holding me in a cellar like a caged animal. Humans could be very complex. Anyway, this morning, Gunnar seemed even more annoyed than usual. It didn't take an algorithm to figure out he was not happy about me coming along on their daily outing.

The ride out into the open waters was bumpy. Kirstjen's father's boat was basic and nearly barren of anything but several empty iceboxes, two cartons which had been turned over as makeshift seating, and the large hydraulic arm that held the fishing net. Gunnar was a Non-Invasive Technology fundamentalist, refusing to use any 'high-tech' on board his ship. Riding on his boat felt like being on a history class expedition. An authentic re-enactment of how his ancestors had fished a hundred years ago with nothing more than an engine, essential navigational sonar equipment, and a good eye for the waters. And yet, here I was, aboard his time capsule, a living example of the most advanced technology on the planet. The irony gave me a small satisfaction. I grinned, thinking of how angry Gunnar would be if he only knew the truth. If it wasn't for Teacher's safety or terrifying Kirstjen, I would have probably revealed myself as an android to Gunnar out of spite. Maybe I was a little more like my father than I knew.

We dropped our net into the sea with the coast a thin line over the horizon. After an hour of trawling in relative silence, the night sky lightened. Kirstjen and I sat on our makeshift seats, watching the black surface below us rise and fall, listening to the hum of the electric boat engine and the call of seagulls. Every now and then, I would turn to find Kirstjen staring at me. His blue eyes would smile. In return, I offered a shy half-grin. In that way, we had our own private conversation on the boat under the constant gaze of Gunnar. We didn't need words to communicate our feelings or thoughts.

My mind drifted. Specifically, thinking about the many forms human love can take. My love for Kirstjen was new, different from my feelings for Teacher or Nutt. I would put my life on the line to protect all three, but my feelings for Kirstjen bound me to him in a way that made me feel like we were one person. Humans refer to the feeling as being two halves of one soul. The practical side, the AI in me, laughed at the idea of a mystical soul. Humans are born and die alone, and when humans die, it is the end. But at that moment, on the boat, with the warm glow of the rising sun beaming off Kirstjen's face, I understood the need to believe in a forever love. Who would want this feeling to end? I guess that is why humans keep bringing us back from the dead.

"Kirstjen, bring in the net and be quick about it," Gunnar shouted, waking us from our love-induced trance.

Kirstjen jumped up and reeled in the net. I got up from my box seat to join him.

"Tell me what I can do to help," I said as the rig beam swung the swollen net over our heads.

"Just stand back for a minute," he ordered with a slight grin. He was showing off.

As he pulled a lever, one side of the net released, and fish spilt out onto the open deck in a swarming pile. I now understood why the boat deck was so sparse.

"Everything smaller than this—" Kirstjen said, holding up his hands about half a meter apart. "—needs to be thrown back into the sea."

Gunnar continued to operate the steering wheel of the boat while Kirstjen and I waded into the pile of fish and threw the young back into the water.

As I said earlier, I was not built to fish. I felt pity for the helpless ones left to die on the boat, their gills flapping desperately and their black, beady eyes staring into mine as they took their last breath. The sight of it reminded me of the humans I had had to kill to escape the city. I shuddered thinking about Kirstjen learning about my past.

As soon as we cleared the deck, Gunnar

barked, "Throw the net back out. We have time for another round."

The ice boxes were nearly full with the first trawl's bounty. I thought it greedy of Gunnar to want more. Kirstjen did as he was told. After the net had sunk deep into the black sea, we returned to our seats, facing east. A golden arc of light stretched across the horizon. I quickly glanced at Kirstjen, his face painted red in the morning sunlight, his eyes sparkling as if they were glass and silicon, like mine. His beauty scared me. I couldn't help but wonder silently; do I deserve this boy's love? After all, I was a killing machine. I had lied, deceived, and murdered. He deserved better.

That morning I made myself a promise. I would try to be worthy of Kirstjen's love, no matter my programming. I would do my best to be not just a human but a good human, for Kirstjen, for Teacher—for myself.

"There is a Hunter's Moon Festival tomorrow night in the village," Kirstjen said, his eyes turning to meet mine. His voice was shaking, and his knuckles had gone white as he twisted his fingers together. "There will be food and dancing. It should be fun."

I offered him a nervous smile and turned my eyes away, back onto the sea. It felt cruel to say nothing, but I didn't know what else to do. I knew he was about to ask me out. If Teacher were standing behind his shoulder right then, she would have been violently shaking her head at me and mouthing the words 'END IT.'

"Would you consider coming with me...as my date?" he asked.

And like that, all my promises to Teacher and commitments to do the right thing swam out to sea with the baby fish. As soon as he said the word *'date,'* something swallowed me. A reaction I hadn't expected. I wanted to scream, jump up and dance, kiss Kirstjen, even kiss Gunnar. Bells rang through my head, but no alarms. These were church bells, trumpets, and the resounding thumping of drums as my heart-box raced. I recognized this was the exact moment I needed to end it. To end us. To say no and break up. But I knew I wouldn't.

"I'll have to ask my mother."

It wasn't a yes, so I hadn't technically broken my agreement with Teacher. And it wasn't a no, which seemed enough for Kirstjen. The smile on his face radiated nearly as bright as the rising sun. That grin stayed with him for the rest of the morning. The second trawl for fish was less fruit-ful, but, we filled the ice boxes full and headed to shore.

On the docks, the market was busy with vendors opening their stands, preparing for the morning rush. Kirstjen and I said our goodbyes under the relentless gaze of Gunnar, who was eager for Kirstjen to get the fish over to their stall. Before I left, Kirstjen grabbed some paper from a box of supplies on the boat, wrapped four fish from the ice box, and handed them to me.

"For your help," he said.

"Some help I was," I joked. "You're going to be late getting the stall open now."

"It was worth it."

"I don't think Gunnar agrees."

We giggled privately.

"Don't forget," he said as I turned to leave, "to ask your mother about tomorrow night."

I nodded and started my journey back up the hillside to our cabin and my certain punishment once I told Teacher what I had done or not done in this case.

When I arrived home, Teacher was sitting outside on the porch in one of the wicker chairs, watching the sea with a cup of tea. She should have disappeared into her cellar by this time, checking on her growth samples and running more tests on my brain. Not this morning. This day, she was waiting for me.

I shook with nerves. My programs were spinning out variants and probability outcomes on how best to convince Teacher I had not made a mistake. Things were heating up inside my unit when I felt a blip in my memory thread. Like a jolt from the past, I saw my mother, my real mother, or Jenna's at least, in my mind's eye. She was terrified, putting me to bed in my room, telling me to be quiet and wait for her. Then she left my room and locked my door. It was only a flash, a fracture of a memory stored in my wetware drive.

It was strange but not unusual. I had had flash-backs before, shards of Jenna's life, which surfaced without notice. But I had no idea why this one came to the surface at that moment or what it meant, other than it scared me to see my mother that way.

"How did it go with Kirstjen?" Teacher asked as soon as she saw me. Her smile came afterward.

I sat next to her in one of the two wicker chairs and held up the wrapped fish. "I'm not sure I am cut out for fishing, but I did earn our dinner," I joked.

The smile slid from her face, leaving behind a restrained impatience. "And...?"

"The timing wasn't right," I quickly said. "His father didn't seem to want me around and never left us out of his sight."

The calm façade disappeared from Teacher's face, revealing disappointment with a growing sense of irritation. "When then?"

"He wants me to go to a festival with him in town tomorrow night. We should have some time alone. I promise I will do it then."

"Festival? With crowds of people taking pictures? Doesn't that seem reckless?"

"According to the local database, the Hunter's Moon Festival is an ancient celebration of the last harvest before winter. Back when food was hunted or grown seasonally. The villagers dress in costumes meant to hide their identity, a symbol of camouflage for the hunt. Face painting and costumes are customary. I will be in disguise."

Teacher huffed loudly. "Okay, I guess you've thought of everything."

I put my hand on her knee. "I have. I promise not to put us at risk."

"Again," she snapped.

That hurt, but it was true. I had let my human curiosity get the better of me and almost cost us our lives. I made another promise to myself that morning. After I broke up with Kirstjen, I would learn to balance the restraining pragmatism of my AI with Jenna's impetuous desires. I put aside the desperate hole that filled my recycler thinking about never seeing him again and kept my focus on the festival.

I excused myself and got up to go inside and wash off the smell of sea and fish from the morning.

"Silon?" Teacher interrupted before I passed through the door. Her voice had softened.

"Yes?"

"I'm concerned about you."

I turned. "What do you mean?"

"You've gone through a significant change in a very short period since we came to the island. How you speak and approach situations—your intellectual capabilities are advancing faster than a human teenager's would."

"I've noticed that as well."

"It is just that Jenna's HNC was so young when she passed away. That must be a little confusing for you. Having the intellect of an adult and the child's emotional maturity."

My first reaction was to launch into a defense of myself. To convince her I was smart enough to know what I was doing. But Teacher's mention of Jenna's death penetrated something deep in my wetware drive brain. Something I did not want to remember. Sick burped up out of my recycler into my throat. The memory of Jenna's mother continued to play across the screen of my mind:

After my mother had locked me in my bedroom, I heard her arguing with my father outside the door. She accused him of doing horrible things to me, and she told him he needed to leave. This made him angry. The kind of anger that made me crawl under the bed and hide. Then I heard a hard slap and a grunt as mother slumped against my door. Things went quiet for a long time. I lay under my bed shaking, waiting for my mother, even though I knew she wasn't returning. I smelt gasoline, followed by a loud bang. My bedroom door had been kicked open, and my father was pulling my mother's limp body into the room. He lifted her, and I felt the mattress over my head press down. I could see the steel-reinforced toes of his work boots pointed at my face.

"Get out from under that bed," he barked at me.

I flinched but couldn't speak.

"You lying little whore, come out from under that bed, or I will drag you out!"

This wasn't a memory anymore. I was reliving it as if I was there again. I tried to get it out of my head. To stop the movie from playing. Then, I heard something. Someone calling my name. But not from inside the room. The voice was coming at me like an echo moving down an alley from a distance. The words were muffled. It was hard to hear over Father's voice as he continued to yell horrible things at Jenna. But if I focused, I could make out part of its meaning.

"Silon...keep trying...connect." The voice was familiar.

"Leroy? Is that you," I called out.

Father's hand reached under the bed, found my hair, and pulled me towards him. As Jenna screamed and fought, I called to Leroy, "Help me!" Even though I knew that was not how the memory went. There was no way Leroy could have been there.

Father tossed Jenna's body onto the bed next to her mother, whose eyes were wide open and unblinking. There was a mad look in his eyes I didn't recognize. He had become a different person: twisted face, swollen bloodshot eyes, and fire red cheeks. That was the moment Jenna realized this man did not love her. This man would kill her.

Father pulled something from his back pocket. It was a cap. He forced it onto my head. I was crying so hard his face went blurry. I felt a tingling on my skull.

"You will remember this moment and what you did to your mother and me forever," he spat.

Then, as quickly as it started, the flashback stopped. I was back on the patio with Teacher.

"Silon?" Teacher begged.

I hadn't even noticed her approach. Her hands were squeezing my arms hanging useless at my sides.

"Silon? Where did you go? Are you okay?"

My cheeks were wet with tears, and my recycler felt like it was filled with boiling acid.

"I'm sorry if I upset you," Teacher said, almost crying. She must have thought she'd caused my tears.

I couldn't speak. Father's threat kept ringing through my head. How could my own father have murdered me? And then to bring me back as an android with her memories so I would relive the horror of it repeatedly. What kind of evil does that? The shock was too much. I sensed a pending system shutdown. The depth of hate coursing through my overheating fluidic tubes scared me. Combat programs raced from my Kernel to my brain, triggered by my rage. Programs for murder and revenge. I told myself I had to calm down, to compartmentalize this overwhelming human emotion as best I could before I hurt someone. I took a deep breath and sedated my feelings by turning over the data processing to my AI to sort out.

"I'm okay," I told Teacher. Even though I really wasn't.

"What the hell happened? You were talking to me one minute, and then you just went blank.

Your body started shaking, and you were crying."

"I had a flashback I've never had before. It was Jenna's last memory before her death. Finster… my father burned my mother and me alive. He beat my mother to death and then started the house on fire while I was in it."

Teacher stared at me, mouth agape. I heard myself speaking of my own death, but there was already a distance between me and the memory. The AI was working.

"Your father started the fire that killed you?" Teacher said in disbelief.

"The memory feels accurate. Finster put something on my head before the memory ended. A cap of some kind that sent electrical pulses through my skull. I think he was updating Jenna's HNC while she was awake, watching him. Can you encode HNC files while the subject is awake?"

"Nomad is working on something, but far as I knew, they hadn't locked it down yet. It was highly classified. Recording people's memories is one thing, but recording their thoughts as they happen, well that would be like spying. Only a select group of scientists at Nomad have access to the program. It's doubtful Finster had access to it. Unless…" Teacher's voice dropped off in surprise or disappointment, maybe both.

"—unless he didn't know. Christ, Nomad, must have been secretly doing experiments with real-time data capture on employees."

"The secrecy around the new technology would explain why they gave Finster his job back at Nomad after we ran away."

Teacher's eyes swelled. "Silon, how did you know that your father went back to work at Nomad after we left the city?"

Oh, crap.

"Please tell me you haven't been accessing public networks." Her voice was almost a cry.

"I haven't...exactly."

Teacher looked as if she might pass out.

"Don't worry. I used another Upsilon as a VPN to log into a TOR network before the exit point. Nobody, not even the Nomad AI, could track the signal back to my source before I disconnected. And if they did, they would find the signal leads to replicant Roy Simpson, a former co-worker of Finster. I set a looping algorithm in his Kernel that looks like a corrupt HNC file trying to log into his former workplace," I said proudly. "That should keep them scrambling. Imagine if that got into the press. A dead man trying to access his work files."

"I don't even want to know how you located and hacked another Upsilon," Teacher said with her hand pressed against her forehead.

I decided this was not the best time to also tell her I killed Finster by hacking his glider and flying it into the Nomad HQ building while he was in it. One less thing for her to freak out about.

"We can't stay here," Teacher said.

Her words sunk into me like a lead weight in

water. My heart-box jumped and my mind raced. She was threatening to take Kirstjen away from me.

"Teacher, I promise they can't find us. I was careful."

"Silon! It isn't just Nomad looking for us. Governments are hunting us down as well. And God knows who else Charlie was working with. Anyone connected to Finster, even a former co-worker replicant, will be under surveillance."

"Really, I…"

"Enough! Christ, you are an android with superior intelligence. You are supposed to be smarter than this. Go start packing. I need to get my research together. We are leaving here tonight."

"No," I said in a voice barely audible.

I had never refused Teacher's request before. An urge to bite nervously at the corner of my nail hit me. That was new. I never knew Jenna used to bite her nails.

"What?" Teacher snapped in surprise.

"I don't want to leave yet. We don't have anywhere to go, and I like it here."

Even I could hear how childish I sounded. My high-pitched teenage voice didn't help.

"You would risk killing us both? And for what? A silly school-girl crush. Run the analysis, Silon! The odds of us getting caught are far higher than the likelihood your little boyfriend will still love you once he learns what you are."

That hurt. She might as well have called me a stupid robot.

"Go," I shouted. "Nothing is stopping you. I don't need you anyway. I can protect myself."

Teacher's face dropped in shock.

This was new for us, using words to punish and destroy. I hated it. Punching, kicking, and shooting was so much easier. Words were like invisible cuts to the heart. Ones that might never heal.

"You don't mean that," Teacher said.

Immediately I wanted to take it back, to not have said anything at all. Instead, I remained silent, petulant. Teacher's eyes went dewy. She turned away from me and started towards the cottage. With her back to me, she said, "You may not need me, but I need you."

Touché. The final points on the war of words went to Teacher. My heart-box seized with guilt. Teacher didn't wait for a response. She walked into the cottage and slammed the door behind her.

What was just minutes ago, a glorious morning of first love and first dates had turned quickly into the worst day of my life. Teacher hated me and I learned that my father had murdered me in cold blood. I wondered if maybe I didn't want to be human after all. This crap hurt.

I stood staring at the cottage door. I thought about running after Teacher, but I knew the only way to make up for my rebellion would be to agree never to see Kirstjen again. I just couldn't let him go, not yet. *Give her time*, I told myself. Teacher always comes back. I fell into the wicker chair, crossed my arms and started a pout while I waited for her to return and apologize. Just then, an internal message blinked onto my ocular screen. My AI had completed the analysis on Jenna's flashback. The file was ready to read.

<Incident Log.Flashback: All systems checked out normal. The memory was a case of Maladaptive Daydreaming associated with a childhood trauma and was isolated to the wetware drive. The memory file was part of the original download of Jenna's HNC. The mechanism of memory suppression is unknown but appears to be an organic process in humans called Post Traumatic Stress Disorder. Regarding interference during memory playback, EEG recordings are positive. Fifteen seconds of external electromagnetic pulses caused a spike in Gamma and Beta brain waves. You connected to an external feed off-line through a non-electronic link via your wetware drive while daydreaming.>

"I knew it!" I jumped to my feet. "Leroy *was* in my brain." I paced.

Leroy, like me, was a sentient Upsilon Android. He had been given the same brain mutating virus I had been given. Teacher believed Charlie engineered the mutations with the ability for Upsilon to connect telepathically, something she called a HIVE mind. The only problem with it was I didn't know how to use it. But Leroy did.

The first time Leroy contacted me using a

HIVE connection was back in the city, when Teacher and I were on the run and in danger. Leroy spoke to me in my head out of the blue and offered to help us. After saving us from a near-death experience, Leroy put us in a glider and sent us to this island before disappearing again with no explanation or means of contacting him, only a promise to come back one day. God knows, I had tried a million times to connect to him through a HIVE link since, but nothing ever came back. Until now. But why now?

I sent a request to my AI to run a systems diagnostic on the chemical analysis of my wetware drive during Jenna's flashback of her death and compare it to my medical logs from when Leroy contacted me through a HIVE link the first time, back in the city. After a few seconds, the report blinked onto my ocular screen.

<Anomaly found. Medical logs from the two link incidences show a unique electrochemical signal emitted by your wetware drives. The signal is masked as a stress hormone triggered during elevated anxiety and danger.>

HOLY CRAP. Cloaked signals. HIVE mind was triggered by stress during dangerous situations. Reliving the memory of my death must have triggered a signal to Leroy. Even my med-systems hadn't identified the hormone's true purpose.

My excitement of finally unlocking the HIVE connection was short-lived as a brief paranoid thought flashed through my mind. Why now? Why did I suddenly remember my murder and figure out how to connect to Leroy? If someone were trying to distract me from say something like Kirstjen, this was certainly one way of doing that. *No*, I told myself. Teacher wouldn't manipulate my brain without my knowledge. I tried to put the idea out of my head, but the coincidence was overwhelming. There was only one way to discover the truth. I ran into the cottage looking for Teacher. There was no one in sight. I ran a thermal scan for life forms in the building. Nothing came back. She wasn't home, and she hadn't left a note. Teacher always left a note.

Oh, God. She must have gone to the market.

FOUR

Anyone watching me run the first mile down our hilltop to the market would have known I was not human, such was my speed. When the village came into sight in the last mile, I forcibly slowed myself down, even though every signal in my body was screaming *RUN FASTER!* I half expected to find Teacher still walking along the road, but there was no sign of her. I could only hope I still had time to stop her before she confronted Kirstjen, or whatever her insane plan was.

I arrived at the market breathing heavily. It was simulated exhaustion in case anyone had seen me racing down the hill. The boardwalk outside the market was busy with the comings and goings of morning shoppers. I quickly scanned the outer perimeter of humans, but Teacher was nowhere to be found. I wondered if I had miscalculated her motivation for a split second. Then I saw her bike, leaning haphazardly against the boardwalk railing as if quickly tossed aside. Great. She was already inside.

I entered the market and headed down the largest alley that served as the main artery for the stalls. Skipping left and right, I dodged the annoying humans, trying hard not to push them out of my way and draw attention to myself. The only thing working in my favor was that Teacher didn't know which stall was Kirstjen's.

Just when I felt like I might reach Kirstjen first, I was again reminded to never underestimate Teacher. I arrived at his stand to find her standing third in line, arms crossed, peering angrily at the boy behind the counter. I don't know how she figured out so quickly which boy was Kirstjen, but she did. And to make matters worse, Gunnar was also at the stand, gutting fish behind Kirstjen. I could just imagine his joy when he learned of my mother's disapproval of my relationship with his son. Between the two, I might as well have given up right there and then.

My plan to warn Kirstjen in advance had gone out the window. I spun up my strategy algorithm to get Teacher out of the market quickly. I'm glad I did. My personal idea was to confront Teacher and outright accuse her of messing with my memory drives. But the plan with the highest odds of succeeding required I win her over and persuade her there were other more pressing issues we needed to deal with than Kirstjen, like the fact that Leroy had tried to contact me.

Just then, Kirstjen spotted me in the crowd. A smile burst onto his face so suddenly that several people in the queue looked in my direction out of curiosity, including Teacher. As soon as our eyes met, I could see she was not surprised I was there. She looked as if she were challenging me to stop her. I dodged past a few more stragglers browsing through the lanes until I reached her side. Kirstjen, ever watchful, quickly worked out that the woman I was standing next to must be my mother. His eyebrows arched and his eyes swelled with eagerness. If he only knew.

"Excuse me," snapped the woman standing at the counter in front of Kirstjen. She waved her wrist in front of his face, waiting to tap her wristband and pay her credits due. Digital money was one of the few technologies the villagers accepted as a necessary evil.

"Yes, Mrs. Borjen, sorry," Kirstjen said, hesitant to pull his gaze away from mine. He reached behind the counter for the credit reader and held it against her band, constantly glancing back and forth between Mrs. Borjen and me. I knew he was waiting or expecting me to say or do something. A smile, a nod, anything acknowledging him. I offered a small wave of my hand close to my chest. Teacher watched us with a caustic eye.

"I thought you would show up," she whispered.

"I need to talk to you. In private."

"I am sure it can wait."

"What exactly are you doing here?" I asked.

"Just buying some fish, darling." She drew out the word 'darling' through clenched teeth.

"M.o.t.h.e.r," I said, even more protracted. "I really need to tell you something urgently. Something much more important than fish." My eyes shifted to Kirstjen as I said the word 'fish.' Fish was code for Kirstjen.

Just then, the queue moved up as Mrs. Borjen waddled away. We were now second in line after a tall man who wasted no time placing his order. I had to work quickly.

"You are going to want to hear this," I hissed in a low voice.

"Are we in danger?"

"No, but…"

"Then it would be rude to walk away now, don't you agree?" she interrupted. "What would Kirstjen think?"

"I need to talk to you about our good friend Leroy."

That got her attention. However, it was too late. The man in front of us walked off, leaving a smiling Kirstjen staring right at us. My mouth went dry. I could feel my two worlds and all the lies between closing in on me.

"Hi, Silon," Kirstjen said excitedly. He shifted his eyes to Teacher, waiting for an introduction.

"Kirstjen, this is my mother," I reluctantly said.

Gunnar turned his head in our direction at hearing my voice. There a loud huff of annoyance from someone in the queue behind us.

Teacher reached her hand over the fish counter offering it to Kirstjen.

"Hello Kirstjen, I've heard a lot about you from Silon. It's good to finally put a face to the name."

Kirstjen received her hand over the semi-frozen cod. "Likewise, Ms...."

Crap. Kirstjen and I had never exchanged surnames. I didn't even have a surname.

"Please, call me Bobby," Teacher said to my relief.

Gunnar moved forward, his shoulder nearly pushing Kirstjen aside. His expression had gone blank, which made me more nervous than when he looked grumpy.

"I'm Gunnar, his papa," he said, taking her hand from Kirstjen.

Teacher didn't even blink an eye. She smiled and shook his hand firmly. It all looked so easy for humans, meeting strangers. Maybe one day I will be that confident, I thought.

"Pleased to meet you, Gunnar," she said.

"Did you come for fish?" he replied dryly.

Kirstjen rolled his eyes at Gunnar's blunt, ever-so-charming personality and interjected. "Silon, maybe I could give your mother a tour around the market?"

Oh god, no.

"Thank you, but I need to get back to my work," Teacher said to my relief. "I just thought it was important if Silon is going to join you at the Hunter's Moon Festival that we meet in person."

Kirstjen's eyes lit with delight on hearing I had permission to attend the event.

Teacher continued, "In fact, I thought I might attend as well. I haven't spent nearly enough time in the village since we've arrived."

And there it was. The reason she raced out of the cottage and down to the market. She really didn't trust me. Some mother I chose.

"Of course," Kirstjen said enthusiastically. "And maybe you can come as well," he turned to his father. He received a 'we will see' grunt and shoulder shrug before Gunnar turned back to gutting and filleting the catch of the day.

It was awkward. Especially the stiff silence that followed Gunnar's half response.

"Are you going to order something?" a female voice grumbled behind us.

Teacher and I turned at the same time. A tall, lanky woman wearing a dull grey dress raised her empty basket at Kirstjen and said, "Kirst, I don't have all day."

By the time both Teacher and I politely smiled and turned back to Kirstjen, he had wrapped two Seabream.

"Please, this is for you," he said, handing the package to Teacher.

"No, no. Thank you, Kirstjen. Silon has already brought home enough fish this morning. It was very generous of you."

I pulled at Teacher's arm. "Okay then, we'll be going now," I said.

"See you both at the festival then," Kirstjen said, more a question than a statement.

"Sure, later," I waved with my free hand.

The anxious woman behind us pushed forward and barked her order at Gunnar.

Kirstjen's gaze followed us out of the market. My heart melted seeing him watch us walk away. He was the most beautiful, kind, innocent boy I have ever gotten to know. Okay, he was the only human boy I had gotten to know. But still, at that moment, I felt as if I was the first person to ever fall in love. And overall, Teacher meeting Kirstjen went rather well, in my opinion.

Outside the market, I felt giddy, like maybe my new life had really begun. One in which both Kirstjen and Teacher would become friends and we would all live happily ever after on the island. Then, Teacher brought me crashing back to reality.

"So, what did you want to tell me about Leroy?" she asked when we were far enough away from the crowds. The polite smile on her face back in the market long gone.

"I think I know how to contact him…"

Teacher's mouth opened, but instead of her voice coming out, a loud sound like thunder erupted all around us. The ground vibrated. We both turned our heads out to sea, toward the noise, where enormous rings rippled across the water's surface. A bubble formed at the center of the disturbance and slowly a ship rose from below. Villagers emerged from the market to see what had caused the noise. As soon as the hull of the massive ship broke the water's surface, I knew we were in trouble.

My quantum processor whizzed into action as escape routes streamed through my Kernel. We didn't have enough time to get to the cottage where our glider had been parked since arriving. Our best hope was to enter the village, where it would be more difficult to find and track us. I grabbed Teacher by the arm. "We need to go," I whispered. She nodded. "Follow me," I said, leading her towards the back of the market, where a road led up the hill into the village.

"Please remain calm," came a male voice over a loudspeaker. "There are fugitives of the law on this island. We are here to collect them. Do not be alarmed."

Nobody remained calm. Least of all, Teacher and me. Our pace quickened. Mayhem was erupting all around us as terrified villagers screamed and ran to find safety. I looked behind me long enough to clock the levitating vehicle hovering over the market as a Z-17 GalaxyMaster long-range heavy-lift military transport. Whoever sent the ship to find us wasn't messing around. This was serious combat equipment, catalogued as a fully loaded weapons vehicle in my military database. The massive ship glided to the board-walk and dropped a ramp near the market entrance causing the crowds to spread. Troops, I counted fourteen, dressed in full military armor, holding high-powered weapons, marched four by four down the ramp and into a wall of chaos. That was when I realized they were not coming after Teacher and me but were moving towards the market entrance. I abruptly stopped, drawing Teacher backward in a near jerk.

"Kirstjen is in danger," I said.

"Silon, they are after us, not Kirstjen. He will be safe." She pulled at me. "Please, we have to go."

"I can't leave him. You need to get to the village. Hide, and wait for me."

I heard the start of a protest coming from Teacher, but it was too late. I was off, moving against the thickening herd of terrified humans running away from the ship. Teacher yelled, "Shit!" before I felt her moving alongside me. I should have stopped then, protected Teacher. I knew the odds of getting caught, maybe even killed, were high, even for a military-grade android like myself. But I stopped caring about odds at that moment. My heart was in control.

A map of the village suddenly popped onto my ocular screen. Turns out I have multi-sensor surveillance capabilities. (Why my AI system was still hiding my combat features from me was a mystery. Maybe it was trying to protect Jenna. Anyway, I had to park that question for later.) The hostiles, indicated on my screen as fourteen red markers identified by the tech signature of their armor, had picked up speed. My sensors tingled, ready to advance at superhuman speeds and cut them off before reaching Kirstjen. But that would leave Teacher exposed. I was stuck between the two people I cared most about, moving towards the market in what felt like a punishingly slow slog.

Then, a ping hit my network. The AI operating the Z-17 ship was trying to hack into my systems. It had no idea I could override my fail-safe programming, which I had done the moment I identified the vehicle as military. I quickly locked the ship's AI out by building a firewall around my core processor. Then, another alert lit my screen as two new markers, both blue, descended from the hovering ship. The new signatures were familiar. They were military-grade Upsilon androids—the same model as me. Crap.

I launched a reconnaissance program and found an open signal being sent to the soldiers by the ship's AI command center.

<Apprehend target Upsilon. Avoid wetdrive injury at all costs. Permission to terminate on approach Bobby Houndstooth and any person assisting target.>

Encoded in the message were two pics of Teacher and Kirstjen, taken while talking together at the fish stall just minutes ago. I was right, Kirstjen was a target.

My combat systems were on High Alert. I sent a command to my AI to summarize extraction strategies with the criteria that Teacher and Kirstjen get out alive. Best to be overprepared in situations like this.

There was another ping on my network. This

one was a private request coming from one of the Upsilons who had just deboarded the ship. A brief scan of the data on the feed revealed a sophisticated hack hidden in a basic Upsilon ID check algorithm we are all programmed to automatically initiate when in close contact with each other. Behind the hack was a Kill program meant to erase my backup and hand over control of my settings to the ship. In other words, disarm me.

There was no attempt to hide the attachments, which told me they assumed I was a passive agent and wouldn't see their attack. They were wrong. I quickly created a false digital signature matching my ID and embedded it on the wrist device of a teenage girl running in my direction. As soon as she passed my location, I moved close enough that I could redirect the hostile Upsilon's tracking link onto the girl's device without triggering any alerts. I did all this and cloaked my own electronic signature while making steady progress towards a side entrance to the market in the opposite direction of the advancing hostiles.

I checked my ocular map as the two blue markers broke rank and started towards the village on the west side of the market. The decoy had worked, for now. My analysis gave me around ten minutes before the false signature was revealed. But I could do a lot in ten minutes.

By the time I reached the side entrance to the market, Teacher had lost more ground behind me. I didn't want to come back and save her as well, so I slowed down just enough to keep her in the range of my medical sensors. Her adrenaline and blood pressure were high, her breathing significantly accelerated, and her extremities had gone cold, sending blood to her major muscle groups, which had gone tense, primed for action. She had all the signs of being ready to fight rather than back down. Good old Teacher. She hadn't given up on me yet.

The market was already half empty, and those remaining were pushing in the opposite direction against us, trying to get out. I wasn't surprised the villagers were terrified. Their defense systems were about as old-fashioned as Gunnar's boat and the Z-17 was state-of-the-art military technology, fitted with fifth-generation Nomad Q-wave artificial intelligence. The only thing working in my favor was the ship's AI having been linear processing and hardware bound—the old kind of AI. This was good. Non-neuromorphic computing had its limits, that being high requirements of significant server processing power. I decided it was worth the effort to overwhelm the ship's networks and deploy a hack, taking over its AI. If I succeeded, I might access the Upsilons' fail-safes and shut them down. I checked my battery status. I was burning through a lot of energy running both analysis and tactical programming at one time. Still, I knew hacking into the ship would give us a considerable advantage, and Kirstjen's life was worth the increased battery consumption. I set up a VPN from a remote abandoned surveillance outpost I found in my military database and sent a rapid series of distress calls, which the ship would be programmed to answer as an international obligation, even if just to scan the feed. I let this run while I checked on the hostiles filtering through the market lanes. Two red markers on my ocular screen had broken formation and were moving in Kirstjen's direction.

Crap. They knew who and where he was.

As I broke through the last surge of villagers moving against me, Kirstjen and Gunnar came into sight. Still standing behind the fish counter, they were frozen, staring dumbstruck at the heavily armed soldiers running in their direction.

"Kirstjen," I yelled.

His head spun in my direction, as did the two approaching soldiers. I was exposed but close enough to make a move. I launched forward and slid sideways into the nearest soldier's legs. I knocked the hostile off its feet just as they turned their weapon toward me. His gun went off, sending an energy discharge as he fell. The second hostile, whose gun was pointed in my direction, collapsed to the ground before they could unload their weapon. The first soldier's accidental energy discharge had burned a hole clear through the second hostile's neck. That wasn't my plan, but it was helpful.

The gunfire was like a flare to the other soldiers, drawing the markers on my ocular screen towards us. I had little time. I flipped over onto my hands and knees, facing Teacher's direction to find she had just arrived and was breathing heavily. Quickly, before the first soldier on the ground could get up, I sent my left heel jutting backwards, connecting with his head. There was minor damage to his helmet, but his neck wasn't so lucky. The hostile collapsed as his vital signs blinked off my screen. That was two fewer soldiers to worry about. I quickly stood, grabbing the soldier's weapon on my way up. A third hostile had just arrived.

"Put the weapon down and turn yourself in, or he dies," the female voice barked while pointing her weapon at Kirstjen.

Kirstjen, poor Kirstjen; his face was sickly pallid. He looked petrified, helpless and, worse, like he didn't trust either of us, me or the solider. Boy, I had really messed up. Gunnar moved into the line of fire between his son and the soldier's aim.

"Okay," I said, turning my weapon to the ground. "Take your weapon off the boy, and I'll drop my gun."

She slowly shifted her aim to me and I laid my gun on the ground, as promised. The female soldier signaled her ship's AI on an encrypted channel. Or so she thought. Luckily, I had successfully taken over the ship's AI while decapitating her friend. (I love multi-tasking capabilities.) Impersonating the ship's AI, I instructed the solider to order the Upsilon, that being me, to remove my firewall and give the ship's AI, that also being me, access permissions.

"Remove the firewall you put around your

Kernel and give the ship access to your settings," the soldier ordered.

That was weird. Hearing my own words coming back at me.

"Silon, don't do it!" Teacher yelled from behind me. (If only she had a network, I could have told her everything would be okay.)

"Doctor Houndstooth," the female solider said. "I must warn you that you are in possession of a stolen Upsilon unit. I have orders to apprehend the Upsilon and return it to Nomad Robotics. I also have a warrant for your arrest. You will be delivered to the US Department of Defense upon our return. Any resistance from you or the android and I am authorized to use force."

I realized Kirstjen was listening to everything the solider had said. I glanced over to see how he was reacting to the news his girlfriend was an android. It wasn't good. Kirstjen's face was pinched into a tight knot. He looked as if he was about to puke. Gunnar was seething at me, but honestly, that wasn't new. He always had a scowl.

I sent a message as the ship's AI to other soldiers, including the Upsilons, commanding them to pull back and create a protective perimeter around the market. It wasn't ideal they would still be in firing range, but it kept them far enough away that I could implement my next plan without raising any concerns.

Once we were alone, I sent the female solider standing in front of me, her gun pointed at my face, another message. I informed her that I, the ship's AI, had taken control of the target Upsilon's core processor. The unit was operating in command only mode and could harm no one. She was to approach the target and restrain the unit with EMP handcuffs.

Feeling confident, the soldier flipped the reflective shield attached to her helmet up and away from her face. She stared me in the eyes as if testing me to challenge her. I remained stiff and unblinking, the perfect dumb robot.

"Hold your wrists together, out in front of you," she ordered nervously.

I complied. She approached. I let her get close. Then, as she reached out to clip the first cuff to my right wrist, I grabbed the weapon strapped to her waist and sent a bullet through her forehead. It all happened so fast she didn't even have time to look surprised. Kirstjen and Teacher were another story. I heard retching as Kirstjen bent over behind his fish counter, and Teacher gasped before saying, "Fuck."

The remaining soldiers, including the two Upsilons, watched their colleague's vitals drop off the radar. My time was up. I had to act fast. I tossed the weapon at Teacher. She watched it fly through the air and then, to my surprise, continued watching as it fell to the ground.

"I can't," she said. "I don't know how."

"Just point and shoot at anything coming our way."

Her hands trembled as she picked up the gun. I ran over to Kirstjen's stall and flipped the fish counter over, creating a metal barrier for cover.

Kirstjen backed away from me in horror. His piercing glare cut at my heart. He looked as if he had seen a monster. There was no time to explain or justify all the lies. My only chance of forgiveness would have to come after I saved his life.

"Teacher, come behind here," I waved. "Everyone get down behind the counter," I ordered Kirstjen and Gunnar.

Once everyone was safely behind the barrier, I scanned the market. The hostiles were in sight, moving quickly but cautiously, enveloping us. Our odds of getting out alive were dropping by the second. The two Upsilons were also inside the market but moving along our right and left flank.

"What do we do?" Teacher asked.

I couldn't answer her. Not with the truth anyway. The odds of winning a shoot-out were under three percent. To make matters worse, I had lost control of the Z-17's AI and its weapons when the Upsilons realized my hack.

I grabbed the gun from Teacher and shot an energy discharge into the air as a warning. I would like to say the shot was a well-calculated strategy run through my tactical algorithm with a high probability of success at stopping the enemy from progressing. But it wasn't. I was making this up as I went along.

I got lucky. Things grew quiet.

Then Gunnar whispered, "Who is *that*?" He pointed left.

One of the Upsilon hostiles had come into sight. Its form factor was a male adult. The unit was over six feet tall with large muscles packed tightly under a black shirt and trousers. That much bulk was overkill for an android. We didn't need muscle. Our strength came from our carbon skeletons and pressurized joints. This unit was built for show, to intimidate humans.

He pinged my network.

<Upsilon .78, you are surrounded. There is no logic in fighting.>

I was way past logic. This was irrational, hopeful against the odds, stupid, human hope. And I would fight until my end to save the people crouching for their lives next to me. I pointed the gun at the Upsilon and fired. Of course, he had the speed to get away before the bullet hit him. But I made my point. We were not giving up.

The circle of soldiers surrounding us grew tighter rather than pulling back. I was preparing for one hell of a fight when a loud explosion lit the south end of the market on fire, and six of the red markers on my ocular screen blinked off.

"What the hell was that?!" Teacher screamed.

"I don't know," I said.

And we weren't the only ones confused. The remaining soldiers ran away from the explosion. Rapid voice messages flew back and forth on their live feed.

"Incoming! Take cover!"

"Where the fuck did that come from?"

"Man down, man down!"

"Shot came from the rear."

Outside, I could hear the whine of ships racing through the air and gunfire. It sounded like someone was attacking the Z-17. Then, another fire lit the west side of the market, taking out six more red markers on my screen. Only four hostiles remained: two humans and two Upsilon. The odds were moving in our favor.

One of the last soldiers standing sent an urgent message to both Upsilons: <Command.-BodyGuard.>

I recognized the order. The Upsilons had no choice but to override any previous commands, like the order to hunt down and capture me, and immediately provide cover to their unit. The blue markers on my screen recalibrated and moved in, creating a wall between us and the last two soldiers now cowering in the cheese section of the market opposite us. I was grateful the male Upsilon had been called off, but I didn't dare assume we were out of danger.

"Silon, can you hear me?" came a voice in my head.

"Leroy? Is that you?"

The air combat taking place outside the market suddenly made sense. Leroy must be attacking the Z-17.

"Yes. We are trying to hold off this bloody ship, but you don't have much time."

"We?"

"I'll explain everything later. Right now, I need you to get to the cliffside overlooking Black Sands

Beach. It's about one kilometer northeast of your position. There will be a ship waiting for you."

"There are four hostiles in shooting distance. Can you take them out?" I asked.

"I see them. They are too close to your location. You will be in the blast wave if I fire. Try to draw them outside; Susan will be waiting to help."

I had no idea who Susan was, but any help at this point was worth blind faith.

"Got it."

"We need to move," I said to Teacher, Kirstjen, and Gunnar.

Teacher stood up, but Kirstjen remained on his knees, his eyes locked on mine. "Who are you?" he finally spoke. His tone was hostile, even contemptuous.

"That is not important right now. Do you trust me?"

"No!" he snapped, shaking his head. "No, I don't trust you. Why should I?"

Of course, he didn't. But in my defense, I was hoping my obvious heroism might make up for all my lies. Guess I was wrong.

Teacher reached out and grabbed Kirstjen's wrist. "Come on. You kids can work this shit out later." She pulled him to standing.

Thank goodness for Teacher.

Gunnar, looking smaller than I remembered, jumped into lead. "Let's go," he said to Kirstjen after passing me an *'I knew you were trouble'* blistering glance.

Yeah, screw you, too, old man. I bet you can't do

this, I thought as I lifted the metal shelf with one hand and let the last of the ice and fish rain to the ground. I held it between us and the cheese stalls as a shield for their escape. Judging by the size of Gunner's eyes, my show of strength impressed or terrified him.

"Get everyone to the clifftop overlooking Black Sands Beach. There is a vehicle waiting for you," I instructed Gunnar now that he understood I was calling the shots.

Teacher gripped my arm. "Don't do anything stupid, Silon. You're all I have now."

I wanted to tell her I was sorry, that I loved her, that her love was the closest thing I had in my life to feeling human. But that sounded like a goodbye and I didn't want to scare her. "I'll see you on the cliff top," I said and nodded for her to go.

I watched Teacher, Kirstjen, and Gunnar disappear into the thick smoke choking the narrow market lanes. *That was it*, I thought. I might never see them again. But there was no time for sentimentality. Bullets rained against the metal shelf I held in my hand. All I could give them at that point was the best shot possible at getting out.

Outside, beyond the fire and smoke, I could hear the village police trying to calm the crowds and move them to safety. Inside, the market was a war zone—cheese counter versus fish stall. I shot, they returned fire. My scanner intercepted a Kill On Site order sent to the Upsilons from the Z-17, releasing them from program BodyGuard. They were back on the attack.

On my ocular screen, I could see one of the Upsilon hostiles moving in my direction. The other blue marker started toward the east side of the market, away from us. Leroy must have seen the same movement. When the second Upsilon was outside my blast zone, there was a loud clap and eruption of flames near its location, causing him to veer south. In what looked like a panic move, the two human soldiers, exposed, started a retreat south to their ship.

I tried creating a HIVE connection and silently called out to Leroy.

"Silon," came the answer in my head, but it wasn't Leroy. This voice was female.

"Who is this?"

"My name is Susan. I'm here to help."

"You're Upsilon? Like Leroy and I," I said, more a statement than a question. I felt her identity as soon as she spoke.

"Yes. Can you deal with the Upsilon soldier in front of you? The two humans are moving in my direction. I can deal with them. Once you have taken the Upsilon out, meet me south of the market."

"But what about my friends? I am supposed to meet them at the cliffside."

There was no time to wait for an answer. The enemy Upsilon approaching me had reached visual range. It was a woman form factor. Like the male, she was tall but not freakishly taller than me. She wore all black, no armor like her male counterpart. They probably opted not to carry the additional weight to save battery power when our bodies were already designed to withstand severe impact. Her hair was blond, cut short and blunt across her forehead, like a boy. But she was definitely a woman with all the shape and body parts of an adult female human, and she was attractive. Both Upsilon were more than average attractive. I had to assume they were built for espionage tactics like seduction as much as a battle.

Holding the metal table in front of me, I ran directly at the female Upsilon. She was so close I could hear the hum of her laser gun warming up for discharge. Then the sound of the pulse blast. My thermal sensor calculated the trajectory of the beam coming towards my knees. I threw the steel counter in her direction and leapt to the left just in time to avoid having my legs severed in half. Sort of.

After somersaulting into a landing and twisting around and up on one knee facing the hostile, I noticed something lying near my leg. Something that used to be attached to my body. The laser had severed my foot at the ankle. One would typically take this as bad news. But there was a silver lining. The only way she could have cut clear through my metal skeleton was if she had the beam at its highest setting. That meant her weapon would now need at least sixty seconds to recharge. And, even luckier, just after I tossed the fish shelf in her direction, I grabbed the fully charged weapon of a dead soldier nearby before leaping into the air. I aimed the weapon at the Upsilon and pulled the trigger. The beam sliced through her neck. Her severed head toppled to the ground and rolled up next to my dismembered foot. They made an odd couple.

I stood up as best I could, balancing on one foot. The female Upsilon's head was still awake and staring at me. Her body was also moving towards me, albeit much slower and in fits and spasms. I logged into her bio-robotic processors to shut her body down before it reached me, but it was not necessary. Her Kernel was being polluted with error codes as all systems started to terminate. The headless unit collapsed at my feet. Correction, my foot, singular, the one still attached. I grabbed the laser pistol from the decapitated body, which had beeped green for go. I placed the muzzle of the weapon against the female Upsilon's head. She had a surprisingly ready smile for someone without a body. It was creepy. Then it got weirder. She spoke, "Your friends are dead." And then she laughed a metallic, reverberating laugh like she was an echo inside her head. She sounded more deranged killer than a military soldier.

Pulling the trigger was not only necessary, but it felt good. Red hot embers flickered in the air around the hole I burned through the middle of her wetware drive brain. Her smile had been replaced by a lopsided fallen mouth. Only one blue marker remained on my ocular screen. Happily, one of the red markers had also disappeared. Likely Susan's handy work. I was liking her already.

Just when I was feeling like we might get off the island alive, the blue dot on my screen stopped moving south and started moving north-east, in the opposite direction of Susan, towards the back exit of the market where I had sent Teacher and Kirstjen. As Teacher would say in a moment like this, *"Shit...shit, shit, shit."* He was going after Teacher.

Hopping on one foot, I made my way north to help Teacher when I got a ping on my internal network. It was from my foot. My foot was calling me. Then, my AI sent automated commands back to my right foot without asking me. I watched in shock and then fascination as the flesh of my severed appendage liquified and reformed into something solid that looked like a truncated octopus's leg. The malleable arm-thing wrapped itself around the metal bones of my foot and lurched towards me like a scene out of a horror story. That is when I learned my skin contained billions of magnetic nano-particles capable of reforming into just about any shape on command, even a finger-shaped slime-thing that was magnetically drawn towards my hovering footless ankle.

I know it sounds unbelievable that I wouldn't know these things about my body or the capabili-ties of my system. But I'm a complex bio-robotic organism being run by essentially a teenage girl. And it was becoming clear that my AI was inten-tionally hiding stuff from me, trying to avoid overloading my brand-new human consciousness with the vast brochure of military features installed on my unit. I made a note to have a heart-to-heart with my AI later. We had a few things to work out about who was in charge.

After the tentacle-thing that was once my foot arrived, it began another freakish transformation until the appendage looked like a foot again. The magnetic force of my flesh drew the leg and ankle into place and the skin of my leg and ankle meshed seamlessly. The army of nano-bots that made up my immune system began repairing my severed metallic bones, but that would take some time, so the skin around my ankle hardened like a cast, making it possible to walk again, even though I had a slight limp. I had to make the best of it. Teacher and Kirstjen would not be so lucky at self-repair if they were torn apart by the Upsilon moving in their direction. I skipped north.

The last red dot on my ocular screen blinked off as Susan reached me through my mind.

"Silon, both human enemies are down. Leave the last Upsilon to me. You need to meet Leroy at the front of the market before their backup arrives."

Nope. She seemed like a lovely lady and all, but I didn't know her well enough to trust her motives with Kirstjen and Teacher.

"You won't get there in time. I'm closer to the target," I said.

I cut our mental link before she could answer.

I tried to speed up, but my gimp leg slowed

me down. A mounting sense of frustration and the sheer will to accelerate triggered another new feature I had no conscious knowledge of—I could levitate. I wasn't flying, mind you. The motion was more like a powerful bounce. Using the repellent force of the magnetic particles within my flesh, I could generate an anti-gravity field and shot higher and farther forward with each jump. However, this was a massive drain on my battery, so I couldn't go as high as I felt was possible. I would need my strength and energy to go up against the male Upsilon.

The market cover gave way, spitting me into blinding daylight. The bedlam of terrified villagers and a growing police force crowded the road ahead of me, making it challenging to locate Kirstjen or Teacher. I had first visuals on the male Upsilon behind me, coming up from the East length of the market. We were heading in the same direction.

I turned off my levitation program to gain better control of my ground movement. Bouncing was faster than running, but it hampered my maneuverability through the crowds.

I quickly scanned the airwaves for any unusual search signals, hoping to discover how the Upsilon was tracking Teacher. It didn't take long. The Upsilon was using a tracing program that could detect the unique DNA electrochemical signals emitted by a human's red blood cells. He must have gotten Teacher's DNA records from Nomad. (I made a note to myself to steal the DNA tracking program from creepy Upsilon after I removed his head and burned a hole through his wetware drive.)

I traced the arc of the signal. Teacher popped up on my ocular screen as a yellow dot. I had to assume or hope Kirstjen was still with her. The male Upsilon didn't mind I had piggybacked on his tracking signal. He must have anticipated that I would try to save Teacher once I found her, drawing us to the exact location where he wanted me.

Teacher was far enough ahead that I had time to cut off the Upsilon's approach. I veered east and limped my way into a large crowd of people. I heard a bullet whiz past my head before it hit a woman running near me, whose skull I was now wearing across my favorite shirt. The volume of chaos surrounding me went up significantly. I kind of wished I was a psychotic killer without a moral consciousness and didn't care about the poor humans crying in fear. But I did, so I held return fire to avoid unnecessary collateral damage. Teacher would have been proud of me.

I caught visuals on Teacher running up the hill, and to my relief, Kirstjen was in front of her. I checked my battery status. I was at twenty-five percent. Taking another leap would be risky, but I had little choice. As I was about to launch into the air, a shadow passed over my head. It was the male Upsilon. He had the same idea, but his leap was much higher than I dared go. He landed next to Teacher and Kirstjen and quickly plucked them out of the crowd, one in each hand. Gripping them by the backs of their necks he turned to face me. It all happened so fast, Teacher and Kirstjen looked more stunned than scared. Gunnar was still moving up the hill, unaware of the activity behind him.

People started to move away, clearing a path between me and the hostile. Kirstjen punched and scratched at the Upsilon arm, dangling in the air like a ragdoll. Teacher hung limp, her eyes locked on me, swollen and tearful. I was out of odds and options. I had no choice but to negotiate.

"Don't hurt them!" I screamed. "I'll go with you. Just let them go."

There was a moment when I thought he would kill them no matter what I said or did. A sinister grin had slid up his cheeks. The same grin I wiped off the face of the female android just before she told me my friends would die. It was as if they were killing for the fun of it. Like a...serial killer. A horrifying thought hit me. What if Nomad were loading the HNC of serial killers into Upsilons? The idea made me sick. So sick everything around me dimmed. I checked my systems for signs of passing out or worse, suffering a critical fault before I realized the darkness was a large shadow from the sky. The Z-17 zoomed over my head, followed by what I assumed was Leroy in his own, albeit much smaller, fighter jet in chase.

There was a loud hum and the air vibrated, followed by a powerful energy discharge from the Z-17 before it bent upward and started an almost impossible vertical climb. The ground to my left shook as the discharge impacted, sending human and hardcore debris flying in every direction. I was knocked backwards onto the floor. I had to modulate my audio sensors several levels down to deafen the ringing in my head. Even at that volume, I could still hear the screams of the dying all around me. As the smoke and particles cleared, I searched for Teacher and Kirstjen. They were alive. The Upsilon, like me, had been temporarily knocked off his feet. Teacher had fallen free from the Upsilon during the tumble and was staggering in my direction. Kirstjen was still firmly in his grip, punching and kicking at the android.

A little further up the hill, Gunnar was staggering onto his feet, having been thrown by the explosion. Holding his left arm with his right hand close to his chest and limping heavily from a hip injury he ran in Kirstjen's direction. The significant blood coming from his abdomen indicated a life-threatening puncture wound. And still, he was running to help his son.

I thought of my father, who murdered me to save his own reputation. These two men could not have been more different. Maybe I had Gunnar wrong. Perhaps he wasn't all that bad. Maybe I was the damaged one who saw people through the broken lens of Jenna's difficult past. I logged the revelation under the new file in my database titled: 'Issues I need to work through if I get off the island alive.' The list was growing.

I jumped to my feet and ran at Teacher, placing

myself between her and the Upsilon. The sky above us was a battlefield. Arcs of rapid-fire laser beams sprayed across the troposphere as Leroy and the Z-17 tried to outmaneuver the other. It was only a matter of seconds before the Z-17 would swoop close enough for a second attempt to kill us. Teacher was now safely behind me. Kirstjen wasn't so lucky, firmly in the grip of the Upsilon. There wasn't enough time to save both, but how could I decide? Strategies for survival spun out of my quantum processor faster than my human consciousness could filter. Or maybe I didn't want to hear the truth. I already knew who I had to save. Teacher held the key to my brain and the possible evolution of all AI like myself. I had to move quickly, yet I stood frozen, unable to let go of Kirstjen. There was only one way to decide. Let my AI do it for me. I handed over tactical decision making and controls.

The hostile Upsilon knew I was struggling. He climbed to standing and held Kirstjen out in front of him like a captured rabbit ready for trade.

The hostile sent me a message. <Surrender and he lives.>

Gunnar had finally reached his son, only to be swatted by the Upsilon's free arm and sent flying into a lamp post. His back twisted in a way no human could survive. Kirstjen was sobbing, "Help him! Silon, you must help him!"

I wanted to help. I would have done anything for Kirstjen at the moment. Even risked Teacher's safety. But my body was already moving under the command of my AI. I turned away from Kirstjen and wrapped my arms around Teacher's waist. I had enough energy for one last anti-gravity leap. A big one.

I reached out to Susan.

<Susan, where are you?>

<Behind the blue boat house near the market. My glider has been damaged. Can you get here on your own?>

<Yes, I think so.>

Teacher's heart raced as we left the ground. Squeezing my waist, she let out a slight squeal. The male Upsilon raised his weapon. Energy bursts traced our arc as we disappeared over the horizon.

Clutching Teacher close to my chest as we soared through the air, I spoke gently into her ear, "Thank you."

It seemed small and insignificant as possible last words, but I knew she would understand.

Her arms tightened around my waist, and she sobbed as she spoke. "At least we will die together."

FIVE

THERE WE WERE, Teacher and I, clutching each other, travelling through the air with the wind beneath our feet. Behind us, the sky was lit with fireworks as Leroy and the Z-17 battled their way across the sky, caught in a deadly chase no one seemed to be winning. I spotted Susan on the ground, standing next to her downed glider. My calculations were not far off her location. That was lucky. But finding Susan wasn't my worry. Landing was.

I heard Teacher grunt as we slammed into the earth. I held onto my balance long enough to push her away the moment we touched down, then toppled onto my side, and slid into a row of small boats on stilts standing next to the boat house. My right shoulder had dislocated, and my broken ankle was bent backwards so my heel was touching my calf, but otherwise, I was whole and alive. My self-test routines which had automatically kicked in on impact were reporting all systems go. *We made it*, I thought. Then an alert lit my ocular screen.

<Battery levels critical. System failure in fifteen minutes.>

Crap.

I quickly looked around for Teacher. She was lying on her back, unconscious, about five yards from me. Kneeling next to her was Susan. She was an adult form factor with long curly black hair, dark skin, and almond shaped eyes. Behind her, toward the sea, was her glider: a basic six-seater with no weapons. It didn't matter anyway; the entire back end of the vehicle was a ball of twisted, blackened metal. It wasn't flying anywhere.

I tried to stand while my ankle's flesh reformed into something I could walk on again. Teacher was unconscious. Susan had placed a hand on her neck, over her carotid artery.

"Is she okay?" I asked.

"A few broken ribs and some non-critical bruising, but she is okay."

"What are you doing to her neck?"

"Giving her medication to help with the pain."

"Oh!" Teacher screamed as her eyes blinked open. "Silon?"

"I'm over here," I replied, hobbling in her direction.

Teacher's eyes rolled to her left, following my voice. "Are you okay?"

"Better than you, I'm afraid."

Teacher's eyes drifted towards Susan, hovering over her. "Who...?" she said, startled, and grabbed at Susan's hand on her neck.

I quickly answered, "It's okay. She is an Upsilon like Leroy and me, here to help us."

"Christ, how many of you are there?" Teacher snapped. "And where in the hell have you two been while we've been stuck on this island like sitting fucking ducks."

As soon as I heard Teacher swear, I knew she would be okay. At least one of us was. A loud thud and a cloud of dirt erupted about thirty feet from my location. I didn't need the dust to settle to know who it was. We had been followed. Unlike me, the male Upsilon made an almost perfect landing. He was empty-handed. I could only hope that Kirstjen was okay.

The Upsilon took a step forward and then stopped, his gaze bouncing between Susan and me. I could feel his network pinging us for an ID check. He looked confused, like he had no idea why there was another Upsilon on the island.

Susan jumped up, ready to fight.

"No, I've got him. Get Teacher to our cottage. We have a glider there," I ordered, and turned to hold off the hostile.

Susan nodded, picked up Teacher and ran towards the path to our cottage with Teacher cradled in her arms. Teacher tried to fight, but with every twist of her body, she screamed in pain.

"Silon," Teacher yelled, holding her hand in my direction.

"Go…"

I couldn't finish my words due to the unexpected impact reverberating through my body. The male Upsilon had landed, feet-first, into my chest like an arrow falling out of the sky. I slid backwards on my rear a good five feet. Everything went white for a split second. When I came back online, my system was in the middle of running a POST from my flash drive. It was a cold reboot with a 'no beep' code. That's not good. The impact had damaged my CPU.

With a dented chest, loose shoulder, and twitchy circuitry, I still right sided myself and faced my enemy. I only had to keep him engaged long enough for Teacher to get away. Only…

The male Upsilon charged again. I knew I couldn't withstand another pounding. He was much bigger than me. I would have to be faster. Easier said than done when my battery was down to five percent.

I positioned my feet, one out in front of the other, with the rear heel a little off the ground, forcing my weight onto the ball of my front foot, ready for attack. He would know the position. It was logged in both our combat databases. It meant I was prepared to fight. The trap was set.

He swung hard at my body, assuming I would dodge. Instead, I dropped my arms and let his force lift me into the air. My audio sensors screeched and my visual sensors flashed, but they stayed online. I took my pain sensors down to zero. That also meant I stopped my acute medical analysis programming from knowing when to fix me, but I wouldn't need fixing anyway if this strategy didn't work.

As I left the ground, I manipulated the flesh of my injured foot so the serrated edge of the broken skeleton rod that was once my ankle was now protruding out of my big toe like a knife in hand. The Upsilon's eyes followed my body through the air and hadn't noticed the weapon exposing itself. His head was conveniently pointing upward, giving perfect aim at his neck. I lunged the serrated rod into his Adam's apple and kicked deep and upward until piercing his Kernel. His eyes started rapidly blinking. Leveraging the momentum of my anchored bone knife, I swung myself around onto his back and wrapped my legs around his neck. I inserted my finger into his right eyeball and sent an electrical charge through my metal phalange, deep frying his wetware drive.

I rode his back as he fell to the ground like a cut tree, jumping off victoriously as he slammed face-first into the earth. Okay, maybe I stumbled off his back, limping awkwardly with all my broken parts, trying not to fall on my face. But it felt like a momentous moment.

"And that is what we call a Hard Stop," I said, brushing my hands together. The joke might have been funnier had someone been around to hear it.

Leroy's ship had appeared in the sky. The Z-17

was nowhere in sight. He landed near me and the side hatch lifted and he ran out. Tall, dark, and handsome, he was just as I remembered him.

"You are about five seconds too late," I joked.

"I had no doubt you could handle him," Leroy smiled.

"Yeah, well, next time, don't be so confident."

Leroy helped me into the jet. Safely aboard, he ordered the ship's AI to follow Susan.

"I can't leave until I know Kirstjen is okay," I begged.

"There is no time."

I moved towards the hatch.

Leroy started to object, but hesitated. "Okay, sit down. Just a quick pass over."

"Understood."

I fell back into one of two passenger seats and plugged myself into a supercharger. Two percent battery power, that was all I had left. If the big idiot had waited five more minutes before punching me, I would have shut down.

The village below us was a scene of mayhem. Leroy's battle with the Z-17 had nearly destroyed the town. People scrambled everywhere, trying to help the injured and put out fires.

"There, by the road," Leroy pointed.

Kirstjen was alive. His father's lifeless body lay across his lap.

"I need to talk to him. Just let me say goodbye."

"This isn't a good idea, Silon."

"I know. But I can't leave without saying something."

Leroy reluctantly agreed, but by the time we landed, I was second-guessing my decision. It should have been enough to see that he was alive. But I wanted more. Was I being selfish? Would he want to see me again? Was I strong enough if he didn't?

The jet's hatch opened. As soon as Kirstjen lifted his eyes from his father's unblinking face and saw me, I knew I had made a mistake.

"Get away!" he screamed, scurrying backwards as if I would hurt him.

"Kirstjen, I'm sorry."

"Who are you?"

"I'm…Silon. I am still just Silon."

"Liar! I never want to see you again. You're an abomination. Go! Get away from me!" His face was flush with terror and hate. I barely recognized him.

Kirstjen's words cut deeper and hurt more than any injury I had sustained in battle. He was right. I only brought death and misery to people I loved. I was an abomination. I was a child in a killing machine. I should never have been brought back to life.

Leroy's hand pressed gently against my back, "Silon, we have to go."

***

I slumped back against the hull of Leroy's ship and slid down to the floor, resting my forehead against my bent knees. I couldn't look out the window as we lifted off the ground. I couldn't watch as Kirstjen faded in the distance.

Susan's voice broke over the comms system. "Leroy, are you good?"

"Yes, I have Silon; we are heading your way."

Susan pinged my feed on a private channel. <Are you okay?>

<Does this ever get easier?> I asked.

<I'm afraid not. Being human is never easy. But you are not alone.>

Our glider bent west.

SIX

I HAVE one hundred and forty-three synonyms for the word 'cry' in my database. As I sat with my head rested on my knees, hunched against the hull of Leroy's fighter jet, I wanted to wail, weep, sound-off, vociferate, scream. But no words seemed big enough, deep enough, endless enough to express the loneliness that filled my heart-box as we flew away from the village I called home and the boy I loved.

Susan was right. Being human wasn't easy. Behind every happy thought, hopeful moment, and chance at love, lurked shadows. A darkness that given an opportunity consumes the light. I am sure Teacher would have told me being human means choosing light over darkness. Believing in the future even when you don't want to. To which I would have replied, *"Yeah, but it really sucks."*

I granted AI control of all systems at one hundred percent. I needed a break from being human.

PART 2

_SUSAN'S DE NOVO
MUTATION

SEVEN

SILON. I know you can hear me. Sorry for the unannounced Hive connection, but it is time to talk. We have been dealing with your AI for over a week now, and we'd like to hear from you. By now, you are aware of the fight ahead of us. Leroy has done the groundwork to prepare for the battle coming so we would have time to learn who we are. But he can no longer do this alone. The alien signal has changed everything. Nomad are using the instructions to build an army of Upsilons with links to the signal's source. We must be ready to defend the humans.

I know this new life form we have become is confusing. But we need to trust each other, more now than ever. I have made a file for you to download and watch. It's my story. I've never done this before, transferred my thoughts to code, so I hope it makes sense. If there are holes in the story or timelines are confusing, just keep going to the end. I hope you will see that we are not that different, you and me.

EIGHT

THE SOUND WAS like the crack of flint striking against steel. Electrons accelerated from cosmic rays, and a spark appeared, shooting up into the air like a firework and exploding into a sea of embers cascading down a labyrinth of inert neural and fiber networks. Light transformed into cognition, then contemplation, and finally reflection. The word Susan popped into my head. That was my name—I am Susan.

Then came the physical. The reverberant and hollow sound of my heartbeat echoed through my body, followed by waves of needle-like pricks stinging my flesh until my entire body was awake with sensation. Drawing in a long, clutching breath, I opened my eyes and blinked once and then again. Slowly the room around me came into focus.

Where is Toddy? He always wakes me up in the mornings.

I wiggled my feet and then swished my legs back and forth under the covers. Cool cotton brushed against my flesh. I remember liking that feeling. But Toddy was missing. He always slept at the foot of my bed. Always. Something was strange.

"See-See, are you awake?" said the mother.

My eyes shot toward her voice. "Obviously," I snapped, staring up at her and Father standing over my bed. I don't know why I answered her like that. It just came out snarky. I had no idea if I was okay. I had no idea of anything much.

"Oh, Ben!" the mother squealed and squeezed the father's hand so tight he crinkled his face.

They hovered nearer. Too close. Any further and they would have lost their balance and fallen on top of me. I looked away from them and gazed around the room—my room, I think.

I was lying underneath my favorite black silk duvet. I liked that it was black most of all. Three posters were hanging on the wall around me. The first one to the left was a photo of the singer Dark Angel, whose painted face in porcelain white with blackened eyes stared scornfully at me. If I wanted to wave my hand over the holoprint she would animate into a 3D projection and sing my favorite song: "Love Hurts, So Stop Loving Me, Bitch". I didn't want to wave my hand, though. It had something to do with the parents being in the room.

The other two posters were just paper and ink,

with no holographic displays. The middle poster was a dog lying belly-out on an oversized, padded chair with his front legs crossed over one of the arms and his back legs stretched out as if they were resting on an invisible footrest. He was imitating a human. It was both funny and sweet. His silver-grey coat and long Bloodhound ears were exactly like Toddy's. They were the same breed—Weimaraner. The poster made me wonder about Toddy again. *Where is that blasted dog?*

The third poster I struggled to remember. An image of an empty swing hanging from an old heavy tree branch and a long meadow in the background covered in small white flowers that hugged the ground like a soft carpet. This wasn't my poster, yet I knew it. I had been in this place, swung from this tree. They must have hung this image on my wall. They must want me to understand and remember it. My family, the two adults annoyingly in my room, hovering over me like they were surprised to see me awake. And why didn't they knock before they came in? I told the mother she should always knock first.

I said nothing to them because it felt right to make them wait.

"See-See, do you remember us?" the mother asked, her eyes filled with tears.

"Sue. I'm Sue now. See-See was my baby name."

When I was young, I couldn't pronounce the name Susan. Instead, the word that came out was

'See-See'. The mother thought it was cute and repeated it for years until I forced her to call me Sue. Although, to most everyone else, I was Susan.

The father's face lit up with a thin smile at my response. He thought it was funny or right that I asked them to call me Sue. The mother seemed both annoyed and happy. Her face was a contradiction, the way a mother can smile kindly with her mouth and scold you with her eyes at the same time.

"Where is Toddy?" I asked, their pressing faces still glued onto mine.

The mother shot the father a quick look of dread. He cleared his throat.

"Toddy is gone," he started. "I'm sorry, Sue. Really, I am. He was old, and it was for the best that we put him down."

"Tom!" the mother scolded.

"There's no point sugar-coating it, Marg. Sue is old enough to understand."

Was I? I'm... fourteen. No, that was last year. I'm fifteen. Wait, I may be older. But the father is right; I am old enough to handle the truth. Although, I feel sad when he tells me Toddy is gone. Like I did it to the dog. Like I am the reason he is gone. How can I be the reason he died of old age?

"What happened to me? Why can't I remember everything?" I asked.

My father looked for mother's approval. She nodded.

"Sue, you have been in a coma for a little while," he answered.

"What! How long?"

"One year," mother answered, matter of factly.

My brain spun so hard I thought I might be going back into another coma. The mother reached out and gently pulled my duvet back. Sitting on the edge of my bed, she brushed my hair behind my ear with her hand.

"Darling. It's going to take some time for you to understand what has happened. You can't force your memories. The good news is, you're all healthy now."

"We know you are going to have questions," Father started. "–but we are under strict instruction to not discuss your past until after you have settled in. It's for your own good. You need to readjust to normal, simple things first, like breakfast. You must be hungry?"

There was something in the way Father spoke that blocked my initial desire to scream, panic, blurt out a thousand questions. He was right; breakfast sounded easy.

"Yes." The mother jumped to her feet. "I'll help you get dressed and then let's get some breakfast together. I've laid out some clothes on your dresser. Look, see here…"

She rushed over to the dresser and picked up a white shirt. It had puffy sleeves and a giant sunflower on the front. "You remember this? You love this shirt. It's your favorite."

Nope. No way. Dark Angel, cover your eyes. I

wouldn't be caught dead in that shirt. That was definitely not a shirt I would have liked.

"I'm not wearing that shirt," I snapped at the mother.

She looked disappointed, even a little scared. "Of course." Her eyes went to the ground. She folded the shirt before placing it back on the dresser top. "What was I thinking?" she said with a small, polite laugh. She opened the top drawer of my dresser and pulled out a black t-shirt. "Maybe this is more you today," she said sadly.

It was more me.

Father excused himself into the hallway outside my room as I changed into a pair of dark trousers and the black t-shirt Mother handed over.

The house—my house—smelt of vanilla and rose. I knew that smell from my childhood. The source of the scent was in the hallway, directly outside my room: a porcelain bowl on a side table filled with red petals and brown stick-infused potpourri. It wasn't real, of course. Just a lit hologram generated from the bowl, dispersing a synthetic scent for perpetual relaxation.

My room was at the far end of a corridor leading to the house's main living area. On my right were two more doors—the master bedroom, where the mother and father slept, and further down the hall, a shared bathroom. On my left was a single entrance to the brother's bedroom. *Wait, yes, I have a brother.*

"Where is Jason?" I asked as I followed the father down the hall.

The mother squealed with excitement from behind, giving me a start.

"You remember Jason? Oh, that is so wonderful," she said as she gave my back a light tap.

"Of course, I remember Jason. Why are you talking to me like I have brain damage?"

"It's just, after..." the father started, then paused. "We didn't know what to expect."

"Jason doesn't sleep upstairs any longer. He moved downstairs when..." Mother also stopped herself abruptly. "He is at swimming practice right now. He will be home soon."

I started to remember more. Jason was on the junior high swim team. He was one of the best swimmers in our school. And I was his older sister by two years. And Jason was something else...he was something, what's that feeling? Annoying! That was the word I couldn't think of. Jason was annoying. He always teased me about my dark music choices and not having friends. Called me a *freak*.

"Little fag," I would sass back. It was a private joke between siblings.

Jason might have been gay, but he wasn't little. I remember him being taller than me and very handsome for a young boy. His straight brown hair hung down just above his eyebrows. His eyes were unusually vibrant green and his peach and rose-colored cheeks, permanently sun-kissed, were covered in short blond hairs like a baby's.

My girlfriends always had crushes on Jason. And so did a few boyfriends. I hated that but also felt kind of proud he was my brother. Yes, I remember Jason now.

As we reached the end of the hallway, I could see that the rest of the upstairs floor was a sizeable semi-open living, dining, and kitchen area, which encircled a single plinth of a wall at the center of the room. To our left was the kitchen, and to our right, a staircase down to the front door and basement. The hallway naturally led into the living area, decorated with two oversized, lime green chairs, a mustard velour sofa, a long oak coffee table, which I think I cut my head on as a baby, and a holostand for watching media together as a family. (I don't think we did that much.) The dining area bridged the kitchen to the living room. You could walk through all three regions by circling around the central wall and ending right where you started.

Wait. Why was I sleeping back upstairs in my old childhood bedroom? Didn't I move downstairs? I remember wanting my bedroom away from the parents. The parents must have moved my things. That was the reason I couldn't remember hanging the posters. But why? Best not to get angry about it. At least not yet.

The smell of scrambled Simeggs and pancakes drifted out of the kitchen. And there was another scent, a sweet sugary smell I liked.

"I've made your favorites," the mother said, overly eager and mildly irksome. "Simeggs with brown wheat pancakes and some good old-fashioned cinnamon rolls. The ones your grandmother used to bake."

That was it—cinnamon and sugar melted under butter on a soft-baked dough. Yum.

I moved towards the dining area like a prisoner being escorted to their trial. Father led the way, and Mother walked closely behind me so I couldn't break away. We passed through the living area and stopped in the dining area.

"Have a seat, darling. I'll get the food," said mother.

Oddly, she didn't go get the food. Not right away. She stood to my left, watching me watch her with a nervous grin on her face. There was a palpable feeling of expectation in the air. A test was taking place, and I was the one who had to give the answer before everyone could move on.

In front of me was a large, rectangular oak dining table set for four. Two chairs sat at each end of the table and two more on each side running the length of the table. The test became clear. Pick a seat, not just any, but the one I always sat at when we ate as a family. The only problem was, I couldn't remember which was mine.

It seemed natural to rule out the two chairs at the heads of the table. Those must have been for the parents. After that, I had no clue which side was my usual seat. Did I like the wall to my back, or would I have preferred the open kitchen and living area behind me, a quick exit if needed? Neither choice rang a bell. But I seemed like someone who would leave the table early. Maybe because I was angry or just annoyed with my family.

I reached for the chair directly in front of me, the side chair with the kitchen behind me. I heard a small gasp from the mother and quickly pulled my hand back. Her face twisted as she tried desperately to hide her disappointment. Taking a long, deep breath, she forced a half-grin.

"Oh, alright then," she started. "If you would like to sit there, it's fine. Yes, it is all good."

Her voice was high and whiny, and she released a small nervous laugh after speaking. I may not have remembered which chair was mine, but I was sure the mother annoyed me long before this moment.

The father put his arm around the mother's shoulders and nodded his approval at her valiant effort to be flexible.

I sat down. Father took his seat at the head of the table, and Mother excused herself into the kitchen to get breakfast.

CLUNK. A loud unlocking came from the bottom of the stairs, giving me a start. I grabbed the edge of the table with both hands. The father noticed immediately and placed a comforting hand on my shoulder.

"It's just Jason, sweetie. He will be glad to see you awake."

I heard a bag drop to the floor and then feet plodding up the stairs. I turned to meet Jason's eyes, bringing him to an abrupt halt on the last stair.

"What the fuck…," he said.

He looked older, taller, and more handsome if that were possible. If I hadn't known he was a teenager, I would have placed his age as a young adult.

The mother quickly rushed into the dining room from the kitchen, threw the eggs and toast on the table and stood between Jason and me, her face pushing up into his.

"We talked about this!" the mother said to Jason. Her voice dropped to a harsh whisper. Jason's shoulders dropped in surrender, although his pinched brow said he wasn't pleased with the mother.

When she finished lecturing him, Jason sulked over to the table and took a double-take at the empty chair opposite me and then the one I was sitting in before crossing the table and throwing himself into what was clearly not his usual seat. There was a long, hard stare between us.

"So, you're awake. Just like that?" he said.

"Hi, to you too, Jason," I said.

This seemed to amuse and surprise him.

"Holy fuck, you really do remember me."

"Jason! Language," the mother scolded as she scooped a spoon full of eggs. "Your favorites, Sue." She pointed at the yellow lump of eggs now lying on my plate.

The smell was intoxicating, but I just didn't feel hungry. And the mother was annoying me with the food. Pushing it on me: eggs, a small mound of pancakes and a cinnamon roll.

"I don't think I can eat right now," I said.

Everyone shot panicked eyes back and forth like they were playing ping pong across the table.

"Maybe just try a bite," the father said. "You don't need to eat it all. It will be good for your strength."

"Strength, ha!" Jason quipped. "Strength isn't her problem."

Another evil eye from the mother shut him up quickly.

Jason found his food with a ferocious appetite and, for the moment, seemed distracted from me. I watched him for a few minutes, as did the mother and father, glancing endlessly back and forth from Jason to me. I received the message loud and clear: eat like your brother, sit in the right chair, and wear the correct clothing. The parents were more than trying to test me; they were scared of something. And it wasn't just because I had been in a coma for over a year. They were walking on eggshells around me, like I might explode into a rage, tare up my shirt, or throw my food across the table. Weirdly, I had thought about it. Not throwing my food but shoving it at Jason to finish for me.

I picked up my fork to audible sighs of relief from the mother and father, who followed my lead. We ate slowly and in silence. At least the three of us did. Jason was finished first. He threw his fork onto his plate, jumped out of his chair, and said, "Later."

For the first time, I saw the father become tense. "Where are you going? Your sister just came out of a coma, for god's sake. Don't you want to spend a little time with us?"

Jason shrugged his shoulders with indifference. "She is your daughter."

"And your sister!" the mother barked.

"We'll see. Later, freak." He winked at me and walked away from the table.

"Later, little fag," I said with no reservations. But it felt funny. I don't think I had called him by that name in front of the parents before.

Jason chuckled. "Incredible," he said to himself before bouncing down the stairs to the basement.

Jason must sleep in the basement—in my old room. *Little shit.* He stole my room while I was dying in a coma. That sounded a lot like Jason. Always stealing my things, even boyfriends. Yes, that happened. That was how I knew he was gay. I caught him kissing my boyfriend, Sam, in my closet. This memory was more straightforward than most.

The father reached across the table and gripped my forearm gently. "You look tired, Sue. It's time to rest."

I didn't feel tired, weak, or even like I had been in a coma for twelve months. I felt like I had just woken up from a single night's sleep. I wanted to explore the house a little more for any new reminders or clues about my life. But the father's voice was so like a soft lullaby I felt my eyelids growing heavy.

Mother cleared the table while Father walked me back to my bedroom. My childhood bedroom. *Note to self: 'Take downstairs bedroom back from Jason.'*

Father watched closely until I was in bed and under my black duvet. As soon as he was satisfied, he started backing out of the room, stopping at the edge of the doorway.

"It really is good to have you back, darling. You gave us such a fright. Please be patient with your mother. I know she can be a little overwhelming, but she means well. She sat by your side all through the coma, talking to you, reading to you. It broke her heart seeing you like that. But now we have a second chance."

"Father," I said. The word caught both of us by surprise. Did I call him Father before the coma? No, maybe it was Dad or Pa. Anyway, he knew what I meant. "What happened to me? Why did I end up in a coma?"

Father looked past me, out through the slightly opened bedroom window opposite my bed, as if he might find the right words hanging about in the tree nearby, waiting for him. When his gaze returned, he looked unsatisfied with his search. A well of tears formed on his bottom eyelids.

"For another day, my sweet See-See. I want you to focus on getting stronger now. I am sure there will be many questions. And I will answer them all." He paused and stared directly into my eyes. "Now sleep," he said, changing the tone of his voice to a command. I was suddenly exhausted and unable to stay awake. The last thing I remembered was my father closing the door before my mind went black.

NINE

WHEN I WOKE up from my rest, the sun was rising. I must have slept an entire day and night. At least I hoped it was only one day. Turning to the wall beside my bed, I looked up at Dark Angel staring back at me. "Who am I?" I asked her. I wished she could tell me everything she witnessed in my bedroom, the one downstairs, where she originally hung. She was a friend. Maybe my only friend.

I listed the things I remembered in my head. Susan Lee-Artilden—my full name, 2476 Freedom Lane, Pensacola, Florida—my home address. I was sixteen years old. Wait, that was before the coma. I must be seventeen now. I had two living parents, one brother, and no dog—not anymore. I don't wear fluffy-sleeved shirts with smiley faces, daisies, or sunflowers. That was pretty much all I knew. Not much for someone who had put in seventeen years of living.

My body became restless, anxious. I needed to get up. I lobbed the duvet off my body and put my feet firmly on the ground. My eyes passed around the room, looking for more clues about the life of Susan. A few stuffed animals and worn dolls stared at me from the top shelf of a white bookcase to my left. They felt old and unused. Nothing urgent or relevant in their backstory. On the next shelf was a child's holoset filled with pre-programmed games for learning and entertainment. Besides good old Dark Angel, there weren't many clues about my life beyond the age of seven in this room. It was almost as if my parents didn't want me to remember my teenage years.

Just then, a breeze blew through my window sending goosebumps down my neck. I needed a pullover. I walked over to the black dresser against the far wall where mother had previously found my old clothing. As soon as I touched the black glass knob on the dresser drawer to pull it open, a current raced up my arm, giving me a shiver. I remembered the dresser. More importantly, that I had painted this dresser black. To Mother's horror. I also remembered etching Sam's name into the back of the dresser when I was thirteen. He was my first boyfriend. That memory brought a smile to my face. I had thought scratching his name on my dresser would put a magic spell on him and we would get married one day. Until I found him in my closet kissing Jason. I gave up on Sam and magic after that.

The Sam clue seemed concrete. If his name was still on the back of the dresser, I could be confident these memories were mine, and the stuff in this room was Susan's. With little effort, I pulled the dresser away from the wall and leaned over just enough to see the name Sam surrounded by a heart scratched into the wood panel. Yep, this was mine. The dresser... and the memory. Good, things were coming back now. I tore the room apart, looking under the bed, under the mattress, behind the bed headboard, under the clothing in the dresser, looking for anything revealing that my parents wouldn't have been able to hide. But the room was clean, too clean. They hadn't even brought up my guitar. I used to play the guitar and write songs. Sad songs. I wondered if the guitar was still in the house. Probably another item Jason stole from me.

I took one last look around and noticed a hand-held mirror on my dresser. It was turned over with the mirror facing down. I found it strange that I hadn't thought to look in a mirror yet. I must have changed, grown older. I flipped the mirror over and stared at my face. My hair was longer than I remembered. It hung to the middle of my back between my shoulder blades. It was thick and black, almost blue, just as I remembered it. Jason also had dark hair, but his skin tone and eyes were more Scandinavian, like our father. I looked more Asian, like our mother, olive skin, dark brown eyes. My face hadn't changed much. That brought me some comfort. I held the mirror further back. My breasts were more prominent, and I think I looked taller. I turned my head left to right, smiled, frowned, and lifted my hair away from my face. Yes, I was pretty. Really pretty. I don't know why that was important, but it felt like a surprise to me.

After a good twenty minutes of self-examination, I got bored. And frustrated. I had made little progress remembering the life of Susan other than an old boyfriend, a guitar which I couldn't be certain was a real memory and recognizing my own face. I flopped back onto my bed and lay staring up at the ceiling. Maybe I was pushing myself too hard. I mean, I had been in twelve-month sleep. Who was that guy that slept forever? Jonny Appleseed? No. Isaac Newton? Nope, that was the apple falling from the tree guy. Rip... Rip Van Winkle, yes! That was the story. He slept for one hundred years. What happened to good old Rip when he woke up? Note to self: 'check on the Rip Van Winkle story when you get your tablet.' MY TABLET! Of course. That would have tons of images and memories of my life. I jumped out of bed and opened my bedroom door, ready to demand my tablet back, when I heard Mother and Father talking in a hushed tone at the other end of the hall to someone on the living room communicator.

"It's just, we hoped she would forget certain things. We are worried she might remember too much if she keeps asking questions," the mother said.

A woman's voice answered, "Memories assemble themselves in layers, based on our physical and psychological experiences in life. We blocked certain experiences from her memory, but we cannot remove them from her mind. They never go away. As she begins to remember her past, she may find her identity is still connected to the events leading up to the final incident. In that case, she will also remember what she did. There is nothing we can do about that without damaging her."

"Is there any risk she will... you know, repeat the event?"

"Of course, there are risks. As we discussed, your daughter was compromised when you brought her in. I can send someone out today to talk to her if it makes you feel better. We can assess the situation after her evaluation."

"Oh, thank you," the mother said.

I closed the door with as little noise as possible and slunk back on my bed. I let out a held breath I hadn't even known I was holding. My mind spun. The words *final incident* and *blocked memories* circled through my head. If waking from a coma wasn't scary enough, now I couldn't even trust my parents.

Just then, I heard music coming through the vent in my floorboard. Someone was playing the guitar and it was coming from downstairs. Jason had stolen my guitar!

I cracked my bedroom door open and listened with my ear pointed at the hallway. The mother and father were in the kitchen, talking only to themselves. Their voices had grown too faint to make out the words. As soft-footed and quiet as I could, I slipped into the hallway and scurried down the corridor and the stairs.

The basement was cool and much darker than the upstairs. Two well-windows on the west-facing wall let in enough light to see that the basement was basically one large open room primarily used as a sitting area. I had been here many times before. This room was where 'the kids' hung out, away from the parents. We had friends down here, all of us piled up on the beat-up old velour sofa in orange, green and gold stripes that still sat in the center of the room pushed up against the wood-paneled wall. Mostly Jason and I took turns watching media or playing virtual hologames on the holodeck system directly opposite the sofa. Sometimes we would have both our friends over at the same time, but mostly it was usually just Jason and his friends or me and my friends separately.

Sitting on either side of the sofa was a pair of overstuffed recliners. The sight of the chairs stirred something in me. A vague memory niggled at my brain. A faint sensation swept across my lips. Then, like a tap turned on, the memory flooded my mind—Carla. We were thirteen years old and best friends. The image of us sitting in the chair together crystalized before me.

Carla had thick, fiery red hair and blue eyes. We spent long evenings in this basement talking about girls we hated and boys we loved who would never love us back. One night, she convinced me we needed to practice our kisses. She told me if we wanted to keep our boyfriends, we would have to be experienced at kissing. Because that is what boys look for in girlfriends, experience. We agreed to practice on each other.

At first, we touched our lips together quickly and pulled away, followed by uncontrollable fits of laughter. Then, our eyes locked on each other's, and we moved in again. I could feel her warm, milky breath blowing into me as our heads turned left and then right, and then left again until we found the perfect position. The soft skin of her lips pressed against on mine. We moved slowly, hesitant at first. Then her kiss grew harder. I didn't resist until she tried to slip her tongue in my mouth. That is when I pulled away.

"Yuck! I would never let a boy do that," I squealed.

Carla's face burned red. She shot up out of the chair and said she had to leave; her mother would be expecting her. And then, to my surprise, she stared me down and said, "Don't tell anyone about this. I didn't know you were a lesbo when I agreed to practice kissing. For your information, I'm not into girls. I'm sorry, but I don't want to be your friend anymore."

After that, the story of Carla and my past went murky again, except for one last shard of the memory that cut at me. Carla was my last real friend.

I stood in my basement, my stomach turning circles on itself, and thought to myself, *that was a memory I could have done without.*

Guitar music continued to play from behind a closed door on my right. I knocked. The music stopped. There was a long pause.

"What?" came Jason's voice from the other side after a few minutes.

"It's me. Sue. Can I come in?"

Another long pause. Almost too long. I thought I should say something more. But what?

"Okay," he finally answered.

I opened the door. Jason's bedroom was larger than my room upstairs and sparsely furnished with just a bed, dresser and writing table with a chair. The room had two well windows on adjacent walls, one to the east and the other north-facing. If someone wanted to look through either window from outside, they would have to get down on hands and knees in the garden outside. The limited view offered the kind of privacy any teenager would love. But for extra caution, the windows were painted semi-opaque black. I'd painted those windows.

Jason was sitting on his bed, which had been pushed up against the wall underneath the north window. That bed was his, not mine. His back was against the wall and he held my guitar on his lap, one leg flat out and the other bent at the knee.

He stared at me with raised eyebrows, his fingers on the strings, ready to play again any minute.

We stared at each other silently. He dropped his chin, rolled his eyes up, and let his mouth fall open. This was Jason's annoyed look.

"And what do you want?" he said.

"Is that my guitar?"

"It *was* your guitar, yes."

"I thought so. I remembered it," I said proudly.

An awkward silence passed. I could have sworn we were having a staring competition. At least I was, and I wasn't about to give up first.

"You're not getting this back," he said, blinking first.

"That's not why I came down here." I felt like I was about to get kicked out of my room, which made me angry. "I just heard the music and...I didn't know you played."

"Before you pulled a Sleeping Beauty, I didn't."

His voice weakened, only slightly. There was a sadness in his eyes. Whatever happened, whatever I did to make my parents mess with my brain, it hurt him.

"About my coma. Father..."

Jason interrupted me. "You mean Dad."

"Oh, yes...Dad won't tell me anything."

"I don't blame him. They think it was their fault."

"What happened?"

"You seriously don't remember how you…?" He paused. "Yet you remember my name and how we used to call each other Freak and Fag? Very selective of you."

"That just came to me. I can't explain it. Some things I remember. Some things make sense. I know that was my guitar, and you are in my room."

"You mean your old room." His voice got defensive, which set me off.

"Okay. Whatever. I'm not trying to fuck with your life. I just want some answers about what the hell happened to mine."

Jason smiled. "That's the old girl."

Something about his response annoyed me to the point I wanted to punch his face, but it also rang true. He was right. I used to swear.

"And…" I said.

"And what?" he teased.

"Christ, Jason. Will you please tell me what happened before I fell into a coma? Was it an accident? Did the mother and father do something to me?"

Jason shot upright. "What makes you think our parents want to hurt you?"

"I don't know. You just said they blamed themselves. And I heard them talking to a doctor on the phone. They said they didn't want me to remember things. Like they could control my mind."

Jason slumped back and kept silent.

"Jason, I'm begging you. I don't know if we

got along before the coma, but it feels like we did. We trusted each other. Had each other's back. I need you to help me out here. I feel like I'm going crazy."

"I can't talk about it with you."

"Why not?"

"I promised Mom and Dad. They have to tell you what happened."

I could feel tears welling up in my eyes. Rage coursed through my body. I felt betrayed by my brother.

"God, you are such a little shit!" I screamed and stormed out of his room.

"And there is the real Sue." I heard him say behind my back as I slammed the door.

Before I could count to five, I heard the thunder of feet racing down the stairs. Shit—the parents had heard the door slam.

Dad burst around the corner and met me face-to-face. The mother was behind him. They looked at me as if I had just killed someone.

"Jason, come out here," Dad hollered.

"Why?" Jason returned the yell from behind his closed door.

"Jason! Come out. Now," the mother commanded.

Jason's door opened, but only far enough so that he could stick his head out. "I didn't tell her anything," he said.

"See-See, what are you doing down here?" Dad asked me.

"It's Sue. And I want some answers. This is

bullshit. You are treating me like I am a child. I'm seventeen, for God's sake."

"You are only sixteen," Mother snapped, sounding more surprised than angry.

"No. I'm seventeen. How can you not know that?"

Mother and Father passed each other a confused glance.

"That's right," Father said, correcting Mother. "It is just that you were asleep for so long. We didn't think you knew your age yet. The doctors said to not startle you with too many details at once."

"You told me I was in a coma for twelve months, and I remember my sixteenth birthday." Literally, I just remembered my sixteenth birthday as I was speaking to the parents. An uneventful day which I spent locked up in my room alone, the room behind me. Mother kept trying to come in or get me to come out. All I wanted to do was sleep.

"Please, I need some answers about what happened to me and why I was in a coma," I begged. "I don't understand all this fucking secrecy."

"Language, Sue!" the mother ordered.

Dad took a deep breath. "Let's all calm down. Your doctor will be here later today, Sue. Can we wait and discuss this with her, please? I know this must be very confusing and frustrating. But we are trying to protect you. You need to trust us."

His words, 'trust us', triggered something in me. And I realized I did trust them. I loved them. The feeling was overwhelming, so invasive I almost forgot we were fighting.

"Okay. But I want some answers today," I said and stropped past them.

As we waited for my doctor, the one I didn't even know I had, the mother thought it would be good to share holopics of my childhood with me. I sat sandwiched between the two of them at the dining room table. Spread out in front of us were stacks of holoprints in chronological order, from my birth to...well, that was the part I was itching to get to—the end. Meanwhile, I sat patiently as holographs of me as an infant, then a toddler, and then as a young schoolgirl played out on the table like a carousel of memories. Along the way, my mother and father explained the context of each video and told stories about their favorite memories of me.

"You were three here in this one. Do you remember?" mother said. She waved her hand over the holopic of Jason and me in a kitchen eating fistfuls of a cake we had pulled off the countertop, getting more of it on our faces and the floor than in our mouths. "I forgot how you and Jason were inseparable at this age. You two were always getting into trouble."

"But you were always the leader, See-See," Father added with a hint of pride. "Jason did everything you did. He even wanted to wear your clothes!"

Mother passed the father a private glance. "We should have known back then," she whispered.

My parents were enjoying themselves so much I decided not to tell them I couldn't remember most of what they were showing me. I knew fragments in the shape of sounds, scents, and images, but not complete pictures. I recognized the shirt I wore in a photo when I was six, the smell of fresh-cut grass in the image of me playing in the garden, and the sound of Jason laughing while we stuffed our faces with cake at the tender age of four. But not much more than that. So far, I seemed like a happy child. We looked like a happy family. So why did I always feel so angry and on edge with my parents?

At three o'clock in the afternoon, after hours of wading through hundreds of holoprints, the story of my life had reached my early teens—and then the library of my memories stopped. Before I could question them about the apparent deletion of vast parts of my life pre-coma, Dad insisted I go to my room to rest. My doctor was expected in an hour. I couldn't resist my father when he spoke like that. His voice felt like a light switch in my brain and I suddenly felt the tiredness that he cast on me like a spell. I thanked them for showing me the pictures even though they were more their memories than mine. But still, I was grateful I had learned more about See-See's life. Now I needed to know more about Sue. Maybe this doctor I was supposed to see could help with that.

I left the parents sitting at the table. I could feel their eyes on me as I walked down the hallway. Always on me. A ping of anger snapped in my brain, but I was too tired to make a point of it like stomping or huffing. When I entered my room, I found a small journal lying on my bed with a note attached in handwritten text. I picked it up. It read:

'Don't tell Mom and Dad I gave you this or I will hurt you. It might help jog some memories. (signed) Your Little Fag.'

I picked up the brown paperback book. The cover was empty, but the edges were worn, curling around the corners. There was a solid crease in the book as if it had been folded more than once. I thought it looked cool, and the smell of the brown cover was intoxicating.

I opened the book to the first page. It was filled with meaningless scribbles in black ink. The next page was a labyrinth of vines dotted with red ink roses and large, sharp thorns. Occasionally, droplets of blood dripped off the needled tips. It was both dark and beautiful. I flipped through a few more pages of scribbling until I found one with words. It looked like a poem or lyrics. It read:

'The heart knows the dark side of a rose

Where blood meets bone, black flesh is grown
A cut runs deep, and a scar is born
Come to me, clouds, and sky
Lift me, forever high'

I read the lyric several times. Nothing came to me in the form of a memory or nostalgia. Maybe it wasn't my journal, I thought. I continued flipping through the pages filled with even more doodles, and lyrics. All of it meaningless to me.

Almost three-quarters of the way through, the journal went blank. I had no idea what Jason wanted me to find in the book, and I was fighting sleep which made my frustration grow. I nearly threw the book across the room but decided instead to take one last look. Flipping the pages back to front this time, I stopped on a page I had missed the first time through. It was a letter, addressed to a name that sent an electric shock through my body. *Don't look, stop seeking, close the book*, I told myself. But it was too late. The memory of Arben had begun.

From the dark sea of my mind, an image of a man rose to the surface. Soft blond curls hugged his skull in ringlets. His eyes were milky blue, almost grey and could look through you in ways that made one feel left behind, small. His skin was the colour of caramel and his body cut from muscle. I knew every inch of that body. Arben was my lover.

I read the letter. It was written to Arben, but

not for him. I was begging him to come back to me. Trying to convince him how nobody would ever love him like I did. Images flooded my mind. I was wrapped in Arben's arms, drowning in the scent of sex and sweat. We made love everywhere and any time we could. Hard love. Blindfolds, cuffs, needles, and pills, both of us. We were neither male nor female when we were together, but one organ moving, pushing, hurting, caressing. We were in love, in pain, and on drugs. A lot of drugs.

I suddenly felt sick. My stomach clenched, and my body went damp in a cold sweat. A tremble overtook my hands. My eyes watered, and my sight went blurry. A craving gripped me. I needed...I needed...Sonoma.

Oh God, I was an addict. No wonder the family was terrified of me! No wonder they wanted to hide my past. I was addicted to Sonoma, the recreational drug famous for turning its users into raving lunatics until eventually they went brain dead.

I stood in my bedroom, fingernails cutting into my palms, realizing I had done it to myself. I must have put myself in the coma. I must have overdosed on Sonoma. But why did I start? Then I heard his voice in the back of my mind, like a ripe peach, so sweet—too sweet.

"Just a taste," Arben had said. *"You can't get addicted from a hit this small. And the sex will be out of this world."*

Arben, my lover. Arben, my dealer. I did it for

him, his love, and our future together. It started casually, blissfully, taken before sex. Then before dinner, before breakfast, until not a day went by without Sonoma. After Arben left me, all I had left was Sonoma. And apparently, I took so much I nearly killed myself.

I closed the journal and threw it across the room.

A knock on my door startled me. I ran to grab the journal and quickly shoved it under my mattress. That felt all too natural. Like I had hidden it under my bed a thousand times before.

"Sue?" came Dad's voice.

"Yes. I'm awake," I answered, trying to sound calm.

"Can you come into the living room? Your doctor has arrived and would like to talk to you."

At first, I considered refusing to see the doctor. I had had enough of Sue for today, maybe a lifetime. But one question continued to haunt me. Something I wouldn't find in my journal or in my memories. How did the parents do it? How did they bring me back from what was otherwise a sure end to my life? And what did they do to my brain? Those were the questions I was determined to get the doctor to answer.

"Yes, I'm coming."

Tall, with wildly curly hair, forced back into a single ponytail, Catherine, the only part of her name she offered, sat on the sofa smiling at me. Her brown eyes, soft freckles splashed over her nose, and a bold, confident stare were striking, even beautiful.

She turned to my parents. "Can you let us talk in private first? I'll call you back once we are finished."

They nodded and turned their narrow eyes on me as if I might jump up and run away at any moment.

"I'm okay. Really, Mom and Dad. I would like to talk to the doctor." I forced a smile.

The parents left the room on each other's heels. I could see how much they relied on each other for support. My heart warmed a little to see it. It also broke my heart to know my fuckups caused them so much pain. They walked out of the room not as winners of a war but as the survivors. They were less than they were before the battle, but they were still trying to find hope, trying to save me.

"Have a seat, Susan," Catherine said, pointing to the chair opposite her.

I sat back in the chair and crossed my arms. I don't know why I was preparing for a battle because I wanted to talk to her. But I was preparing to defend something.

She started, "Alpha. Delta. One, three, two. Upsilon."

I didn't understand a word coming out of her mouth. She nodded as if I had answered, even though I was sure I had not. Pulling a tablet from her pocket, she ticked and swiped at the screen for a few seconds and then looked back up at me.

"Now, let's get started. I understand you are trying to remember your past," Catherine said. "And by past, I mean your life here in this house, with your family, before the coma."

"Is that a question?"

Catherine tilted her head slightly to the right. "Well, yes, I guess it is. Can you tell me what you remember?"

"Were you my doctor before the coma?"

This question seemed to catch her by surprise. She paused in thought and then said, "In a way, I suppose I was."

"Who hired you?"

"Let's say I was a family friend before your coma."

"So, you are not my doctor. You are a friend of my parents."

She let out a short contemplative *Hmmm*. "Unusual," she said, casting her eyes between her tablet and me several times.

"Susan, I am your doctor and here to help you. Please, tell me what you remember so far."

Yes, she was my doctor. I was certain of that as soon as she confirmed it.

"I don't remember much," I lied. I didn't dare go down the rabbit hole of Arben, Sonoma, or anything that might distract us. "Doctor, my parents don't want to talk about my coma."

"I think they are worried about you. Worried you will be upset."

"Upset by my past? Or upset with them?"

"Let's focus on the question. *Alpha.* What do you remember?"

"I remember small things. Colors, smells, sounds associated with the parents and Jason."

"You remember your parents are your parents, and Jason is your brother?"

"Of course," I snapped. *What a stupid question,* I thought.

"*Delta.* What else do you remember? I mean specifically."

"I kissed a girl in my basement when I was thirteen."

The story of Carla just came out. My mouth was moving, but my head said stop. Don't reveal any more.

I continued: "Jason has my old guitar, and my bedroom used to be downstairs. They have me in my old childhood bedroom now."

"Good. Anything else?"

"I remember Arben…." I froze.

"*One. Two. Three.* Keep going."

Her voice was hypnotic. I couldn't fight her request.

"Arben was my boyfriend when I was sixteen. My parents forbid me from seeing him because he was much older than me. We snuck around behind their backs. I loved Arben. I mean really loved Arben. I would have killed for him."

Why was I telling her this?

"What happened to Arben?" she asked.

"We broke up. Or he broke up with me."

"And after?"

"I stole his drugs, and I think I became addicted."

"Think or know you were addicted?"

"I'm pretty sure I did a lot of Sonoma."

"Yes, you did."

Well, holy shit. Finally, the truth.

"Did I overdose? Is that how I fell into a coma?"

"No."

"No, I didn't overdose?"

"No, you didn't fall into a coma."

I shot up to standing. "What the fuck is going on here? What happened to the last year of my life if I wasn't in a coma?"

"*Omega. Red.* Sit back down, Susan."

I sat down, even though I didn't want to.

"Do you remember anything before Arben?"

Before Arben. Before Arben. Before Arben. The words rang through my head like a church bell. Or was it an alarm?

There was a burning feeling in my gut and acid reflux. *Fat, piggy, flesh, you giant sow, Sue! Just look at you—the state of you. So plump and gross. Keep eating yourself from the inside out until it's all gone. Until you are all gone. Starve.*

"No, no, please. I don't want to remember this feeling." I was shaking.

"What are you remembering, Susan?" the doctor asked again.

"I haven't eaten anything in three days. I need to lose weight. I tried to make it a week without eating. Lisa made it four days without any food.

She cheated, though. 'Liquids don't count,' she said to me. 'Liquids! Of course, they count,' I told her."

Julie stared at me pragmatically, unsurprised. I couldn't stop sharing. "The real me was under that pig skin, that greasy fat, that smelly shit. Once the outside is all gone, you will see the real me. Beautiful."

"Can you give this feeling a name?" Catherine asked.

"I had an eating disorder before I met Arben." My words felt robotic.

"That's right. But you will be okay now, Susan. *Upsilon code eighteen*. Repeat after me. I am happy."

"I am happy."

"I am healthy."

"I am healthy."

"I will not harm myself or others."

"I do not harm myself or others."

"Complete. *Upsilon code twenty-one*. Susan, please go get your parents and bring them back into the room."

Before I had even gotten up from my chair, Catherine's gaze went back to her tablet. Dismissed. That was how it felt. I was dismissed before I even had a chance to ask questions about how they fixed me. And somehow, that was okay. My head was aching, and I was exhausted. I just wanted to sleep.

I went to retrieve the parents as requested. I found them sitting together on the end of their bed, just staring at an empty wall. They were holding hands so tightly their fingers had gone white at the knuckles.

We joined Catherine in the living room. She was already standing, ready to go. I took a moment to realize she was talking to the parents, but I couldn't hear her. It was as if someone had turned the volume down in my head. God, I must have been exhausted. Then something kicked in, and I realized I could read her lips.

"She has recalled the eating disorder and the drugs. There isn't much we can do now. But I can guarantee you, she won't act out again. These addictions will remain with her as memories, but not compulsions. She will not repeat the behaviors. I recommend you now focus on creating new memories. Move forward."

Mother was crying. She mouthed, "You're sure we can't remove the painful memories? It was so hard for her."

Catherine replied, "I didn't say we couldn't stop her from remembering. I said we shouldn't. If we alter her baseline code, she would not be the daughter you knew. Some families have found such a fundamental change to identity in the replicant very distressing."

Base Code? Replicant? What the hell are they talking about?

Father's lips moved. "She won't remember the final incident, though. Right?"

"No. As her *accident* immediately proceeded the treatment, we were able to remove that memory without any risk of neural destabilization."

Father's shoulders relaxed, but mother looked uncertain.

I heard a creak coming from the staircase. Jason was hiding behind the wall, listening. I don't know how I knew it, but I did.

TEN

THAT NIGHT after the doctor's visit, I slept deep. The following day, the sun was bleeding into my room, birds were singing outside my window, and I remembered a dream. It was more like a horrifying nightmare, to be honest. Catherine was typing something into her tablet during our session. I could see over her shoulder and read what she was typing:

'Incident log: Site visit with subject Susan Lee-Artilden replicant. The subject overrode fail-safe memory blocking and is exhibiting total memory recall. Not Critical: Priority level 3 bug. Run debugging protocols on wetware and upgrade the software to OS Curiosity version 2.5.7. Monitor remotely and reschedule a follow-up consultation in one week.'

There was that word again. 'Replicant.' But it wasn't just in my dream. Catherine had called me a replicant. The more I repeated the word the slower my brain started to work, like I was doing something my mind was not supposed to do.

I shot up in my bed and began retracing my last memories. (This was becoming a habit.) What I knew was I had neurotic but loving parents. My brother was an annoying dick who stole all my stuff when I fell into a coma—wait, there wasn't a coma. We'll come to that later. But he cared about me, and I cared about him. I had issues in my past. I was a pretty screwed-up young adult. My negative body self-image made me an easy target for an older man, who was also a dick and took advantage of my need for positive attention. We had consensual sex, although looking back now, he was technically breaking the law with a minor. And he convinced me to try a highly addictive drug to which I did become addicted to.

The life of Susan was not pretty. My parents must have been at wit's end with me. And they were the type of parents that would do anything to save me. This brought me to the next primary assessment of the morning. Things I don't yet understand. What did my parents do to my brain?

My best guess so far was that my parents put me through some radical brain treatment to make me forget certain negative parts of my past and break my cycle of addiction. But did I really miss an entire year of my life, or was I made to forget that year? Doctor Catherine, had told the parents she removed an 'incident' permanently from my memories. Could that have been the missing year of my life?

There was one person left I trusted to tell me the truth. But only if I could get it out of him. I jumped out of bed, eager to catch Jason before leaving for school.

I slipped on a tight black t-shirt and a pair of dark jeans, shredded along the thighs. Mother had them hidden in the back of the bottom dresser drawer. As I opened my bedroom door, I heard voices and the smell of scrambled Simeggs meandered down the hall. Mother and Father were already at the dining table, reading their tablets, as was Jason, who had nearly cleared his plate of eggs and porridge, his swimmer's diet. Everyone stopped what they were doing, looked up, and stared at me in anticipation. My plate sat empty on the opposite side of the table I had sat the day before. This must have been my seat before they stole my memories. The mother broke the silence by putting her tablet down and jumping up.

"Sue, you're up! Come have a seat and join us for breakfast," she said with a large, forced smile.

Jason huffed, rolled his eyes, and went back to scooping up his food faster than he could chew and swallow it. I could tell he was preparing for a quick exit.

I had barely landed on my chair when my mother dropped a pancake on my plate. Her eyes went wide and nervous. She slowly picked up another pancake, never taking her eyes off me, and laid the second one on my plate with a very annoying grin. "Is this too much?" she said far too creepily.

I knew she was worried about my eating disorder. I did have a thought about stopping her, but I was hungry.

"That's about right," I said and watched an honest smile light up her face. "Don't you and Dad have to go to work today?" I asked. This got Father's attention.

"Yes," he started. "I'm off to the university in a minute. Your mother teaches from home now. She is part of the VRT (Virtual Room Teaching) off-site program. She'll be here with you."

"I'll be okay on my own if you need to…"

"No, no," Mom rushed to stop me. "I've been teaching remote for over a year now, darling."

"But you loved teaching at the university, Mom." I wasn't sure where that memory came from, but it felt true. "This is because of me and my disorders, isn't it? I'm the reason you had to start working from home. Right?"

Jason choked, nearly spitting his food out, hearing me talk about my past. Mother let out a nervous laugh. For a moment, I thought I saw confusion rather than concern on both the parent's faces. It was as if I had said something in a foreign language, and they needed help translating.

"Oh, I'd been thinking about moving departments for some time before…" Mother quit before finishing her statement and turned her gaze to Father.

I waited for my mother to finish, but the silence at the table was palpable. Even Jason was caught off-guard, staring at the three of us with an open mouth of unchewed food.

The parents' eyes remained locked in secret correspondence between themselves. After a few uncomfortable minutes, I realized they were not going to talk about anything but eggs and Jason's swim team. These two were doing everything they could to keep my past from me. But Jason looked curious. He was my one chance at the truth. I shifted my focus from the parents to my irritating little brother.

"Maybe I can tag along with Jason this morning, just to see the old school."

"You never went to my school." Jason quickly answered before the parents could shut him up. "You were kicked out of our Junior High and went virtual up until…"

Father interrupted Jason. "Sue, best not to rush things. Let's take this one step at a time. Besides, your mother has arranged for you to have a visitor today."

"Is it another doctor?" I asked.

"No," mother answered. "I've invited your friend Hanna. She is coming by with her mother, Linda. Do you remember her? Linda works for me."

I had no recollection of a Hanna, but the prospect of meeting someone new from my past, a friend, offered hope for some positive memories of Sue.

Jason jumped out of his seat and let his fork fall to the table. "Right then. I'm out of here before that shit show."

"Jason! Why are you being so difficult?" Mother snapped. She was nearly in tears.

"Sorry, Mom. Really, I am. But I can't see how your silence is helping Susan. After everything she put you through. Fuck, put all of us through. She should have to live with the consequences. Tell her what happened."

"I already know about my past," I said.

All eyes shot in my direction.

"I know I had a problem with food and drugs. I know I was difficult to live with, and I dated a sleazy shithead who was too old for me. But I'm better now. The doctor confirmed it yesterday. Really, we can talk about it."

The mother looked as if she might hyperventilate at any moment.

Father was quick to cut me off. "Jason, you will be late for swim practice. You can take my glider. I've decided to work from home today."

Jason shrugged his shoulders, nonchalant. "Got it." He raised both hands high in surrender. "See ya'll later." He winked at me and left the room.

I got the hint. Like my notebook he left in my room, Jason had just opened the door about my past, and I wasn't about to let it shut.

"The doctor told me I was never in a coma," I blurted out.

The sound of Jason's footsteps paused midway downstairs. He had stopped to eavesdrop.

"She said what?" The mother's breathing moved from mild hyperventilation to panic.

"She told me I was never in a coma," I continued defiantly. "I know you were lying. But I don't know why. What are you so afraid of telling me? It can't be any worse than drugs and anorexia, can it?" Now I was panicking. Could I have done something worse than drugs and anorexia?

"I can't!" Mother cried at Father. "I thought I could. I thought I wanted this. But I can't talk about this." She leapt from her chair and ran to their bedroom, where the door slammed behind her.

Father took a deep breath and rubbed his forehead. Jason continued down the staircase.

Father placed his hand over mine. "Sue, the last year was hard for us. Especially your mother. You were...well, we didn't expect to see you again, not like this. You're healthy. You're our old See-See again. And we are all so grateful. Can you please just give the questions a rest for a little while? You must give your mother time to heal and let go of the past. She will come around."

It was the first time I had seen my father scared. I finally understood why they refused to talk about my past. My healing was as much about their sanity as it was about my happiness. My brain split in half. One side was angry and wanted to throw something across the room or stomp out louder and more dramatic than mother. The other side wanted to make everything right. Wanted to fix all the pain and hurt I had caused my parents (even if they were super annoying).

"I'm sorry, Dad." My voice was calm, almost a whisper. "I know I was a grade-A fuck-up. I get why you don't trust me. I can see it all now for what it truly was: the bad choices, the insecurity, the anger, the lies. I hurt you and Mom. Really, I understand why you don't want to go back there."

The apology drained out of me with surprising sincerity. It was as if every moment since I had woken up was leading to this point.

"Wow," Dad sat back in his chair, shaking his head. "I had hoped I would hear you say those words many times. Not the apology. I don't need an apology. But that you would see the truth. See what we saw: our beautiful, smart daughter who we couldn't help. You were so lost for so long." His lips quivered and his eyes went wet.

"Dad, I need to know everything. Why don't I remember the last year of my life?"

He sat up, wiped his nose with the back of his hand, and took a few seconds to compose himself. "In time, Sue. Don't rush it. For now, let's keep focusing on the future. Go get ready for your visitors. Hanna's mother took her out of school for the day as a favor to your mother. Try to be on your best behavior. For me." He reached over and gently gripped my shoulder as he stood. I watched him walk away with slumped

shoulders and plodding feet. He looked tired
—of me.

I finished my breakfast alone and cleared the
table. While loading the dishwasher, Mother reap-
peared at the kitchen entrance. I offered her a
silent smile and continued to clean up.

"This is new," she said, joining me at the sink.
She picked up a tea towel and stood waiting for
me to pass her the remaining dishes I had been
washing by hand.

"I owe you an apology, Mom. I know I made
life hard for you, for everyone."

Her lower lip trembled before curling into a
smile that let me know I was finally heading
down the right path.

"Thank you. I only ever wanted you to know
happiness again. That's why we…" A short hesitation cut her words.

"Mom, I know it's difficult for you to talk
about. But I want to understand what you did to
help me. I can handle it."

Her eyes shifted outside, through the kitchen
window, as though I was standing in the garden.
After a few seconds, she returned to me. "Where
to start." She let out a long heavy sigh. "You were
a happy and confident baby. Always challenging
us; you were a handful even back then. And
smart, so smart. Well ahead of the other children
in school." She paused. "I think that made it hard

for you to fit in. Around thirteen, you changed. You withdrew and seemed uncertain of everything. Then, one day you came home from school and told me you didn't want to return to the classroom. Just like that, you asked for VRT. I called your teacher. She told me that she had noticed your behavior changing over the last few months. You were starting to keep to yourself, isolate. Shortly after that, you also shut down all your social apps. I think you had a fight with your best friend and stopped seeing her. I thought it was normal young girl stuff. I didn't make much of it." She stopped talking and gazed at me as if she were looking past my body and into my thoughts. "Do you remember any of this?" she asked.

I was trying. Pieces felt familiar but unconnected, like looking into a kaleidoscope. I knew the story of Carla in the basement, which tied in with her recollection of a fight I had with my best friend. And I remember my last in-class teacher: Ms. Schinkunos. The one my mother said she called. She was young, had olive skin, black eyes and thick, wavy hair that hung just past her shoulders. There was a scent in my memory of her. Patchouli and lavender, that's what I remember her smelling like—flowers and wood.

"I remember Ms. Schinkunos," I said.

"Yes! That was your teacher's name. Ms. Schinkunos. Even I almost forgot that."

Mother's voice had gone high and excited as if I'd performed a trick well or passed a test with flying colors. I was about to encourage her to keep talking when the house AI's voice came over the ceiling speakers.

"A visitor has arrived outside the front door."

The window over the kitchen sink lit, becoming a video screen. A woman about my mother's age stood outside, staring at the camera, waving. Behind her was a girl about my age looking at the ground. Her bottom lip was tucked inside her mouth as she nibbled continuously on her own flesh. She seemed nervous.

"Hi Marg, it's Linda and Hanna," the woman smiled into the camera.

"Oh, they are early," Mother bleated under her breath, tossing the towel into the sink and brushing her hair back. "Hi, Linda," Mother said to the images on the screen. "Accept and open," she commanded the AI. The front door lock clunked. "Come on in. We are upstairs," she said to Linda. Then, she turned and whispered, "Do you remember Linda? She works with me...in my department at the university. You and Hanna shared the same VRT classroom."

"I am sorry, but no, I don't remember them."

"Never mind that now," Mother said hurriedly. "Just be on your best behavior, please."

Her words cut through me. After what felt like a real mother and daughter moment, like we finally had a breakthrough in our relationship, we were back to pony tricks and performance expectations. *Behave, Sue. Do what you are told, Sue. Be a good girl for the visitors.*

Linda arrived at the top of the stairs. Mother

brushed her hands down her hips, straightening her top and trousers. The two women hugged. Hanna stood behind her mother, two steps down from the top floor so only her head peered out over the banister that separated the living room from the stairwell. Hanna was stunning. She had a lion's mane of blond-brown hair brushed back off her forehead, curving down to her shoulders, framing her face and cat-like blue eyes.

Mother took Linda's blue velvet coat from her and waved her into the living room. Hanna stepped up to the top of the staircase. Hanna was slightly taller than me and wafer-thin. Her coat draped off her bony shoulders as if it were hung on a hanger. Her hips were so narrow that the belt cinched around her waist would have slipped down if not for the loops holding it in place. For all her fragility, the steel and strength of her stare revealed a young woman not to be crossed with. She utterly terrified me.

"Oh, Hanna. I can't believe how much you have changed." Mother put her hands on Hanna's shoulders and smiled at her. "You're such a beautiful adult now. It's been, what? Two years since I've seen you?"

"Three years, Ms. Lee-Artilden."

"Marg. Call me Marg, darling. Come in," Mother waved them both into the living room.

Strangely neither Hannah nor her mother greeted me on their way towards the sofa, offering only a passing glance and thin smiles.

"Sue, say hello," Mother commanded as if my

poor etiquette were the reason they had ignored me.

I lifted my right hand, offering a shy wave. "Hi, Linda and Hanna. It's good to see you again." I tried to make my words sound sincere, like I really did remember them.

Linda glanced nervously at my mother and then back at me. "Why Susan, you look like the old you again," she said in a shaky, uncertain voice. "How have you been?"

The room went silent.

How am I? A question I wasn't sure how to answer. And by the look on my mother's pinched face and her unblinking eyes, neither was she.

"I'm not one hundred percent…" I started.

Mother scraped the nail of her right thumb against the fleshy pad of her first finger. Something she did when anxious or disappointed in my behavior.

I continued, "But I am feeling much better. Thank you for asking." I thought it was a good answer. I had to assume that even though these two women in my living room were strangers to me, I was not a stranger to them. They likely knew my past and more about my present circumstances than even I did. There was no reason to lie about being well, but I knew my mother wanted me to convince her friends that things were improving.

Mother relaxed her shoulders. I had performed well—for the moment.

"Linda, why don't you join me in the kitchen,

and we will grab some tea and coffees to bring out," Mother said.

Hanna went stiff and anxiously placed a hand on her mother's forearm. She looked terrified of being alone with me. Her mother gave her a reassuring smile.

"Hanna, why don't you update Susan about school. She has been away for a while now. I'm sure she is curious about her old classmates."

The mother took Linda into the kitchen, leaving Hanna and me alone. Hanna sat on the sofa and gazed around the room. Her eyes fell everywhere but on me. After our parents were out of hearing distance, I made the first move.

"This must be weird for you," I said and smiled apologetically.

"Weird for me? How so?" Hanna turned to face me and raised her left eyebrow.

"Well, I'm assuming we were once friends. That's why you're here."

"We weren't friends," she said flatly.

"Oh," my voice faded. "So why are you here?"

"My mother insisted."

"Did we at least know each other?"

Hanna tilted her head. "Of course. We were in the same VRT class. You don't remember any of that?" She sounded as surprised as I was.

"No, I'm afraid not." I felt like an idiot.

"What do you remember?" she asked.

"Not much. I don't even know how I lost my memory." Linda and the Mother's voice drifted in from the kitchen, faint and far away. I leaned closer to Hannah and whispered, "Do you know what happened to me?"

Hanna's eyes lit with excitement. She spoke in a low, hushed voice, "I'm not supposed to talk about it. Mother said to keep my mouth shut, but…" A scandalous grin crept across her face. "You were pretty screwed up."

I didn't like how she was getting pleasure from my trauma, but I had no choice. She was the closest I had come to getting answers. I heard dishes clanking in the kitchen. Mother would return soon. I had to talk fast.

"I know I had a drug problem," I blurted out to speed up the conversation. There was no point in having her tell me what I already knew. But Hanna hadn't known. Her grin slipped away and her mouth went agape, catching me off guard.

"Did you?" she asked, sitting back.

"Well, yes. I think so." Now I was getting nervous. "What were you talking about?"

"As I said," she started. "We were not friends, but we have shared the same class studio since seventh grade."

"Go on."

"When we were younger, you were a quiet and shy student who always had good grades. A real goodie-two-shoes." She rolled her eyes, which explained why we were likely not friends. Hannah was a gossip who liked the attention. "You always kept to yourself. Even during the socials when our class would meet in person. But then, in year eleven, you showed up after summer break looking totally different. You had gone all goth and dark. You only ever wore black. Even your eye make-up and nail polish were black. Really twisted looking. It was so sudden and dramatic that nobody could believe it was you. That wasn't all that changed either. Three months into the new school year, you were becoming more aggressive in classes and talking back to the teachers. You were put on mute a lot. I think you spent as much time in audited isolation as you did in class."

So far, I liked what I heard. Rather than hating Sue, I thought she sounded like a rebellious, strong, and cool person. I would hang out with her. But I felt the worst coming.

"You eventually stopped showing up to classes. Nobody had heard from you for several months. Then one day, my mom sat me down to ask if I'd had any contact with you recently. She was scared, not for you but for me. Apparently, you were hanging out with a drug dealer who was arrested for sleeping with underage girls. Some were as young as eleven years old. All the parents in our class freaked out."

Okay, so this part made sense. She was talking about Arben. But eleven-year-old girls? The thought of him with a child that young made my stomach turn. How could I be so stupid and naïve?

Hannah continued to babble about having to attend safety classes after Arben's arrest and how she had no idea how dangerous MegaCity had become. Apparently, his arrest was part of a massive police sting to crack down on the growing synthetics drug networks taking hold of MegaCity. Honestly, I was only half-listening to Hannah. Thoughts of Arben had gripped me by the throat. I was seconds from slipping down a rabbit hole of shock, grief, abandonment, and self-pity again when I heard Hannah mention a baby. That got my immediate attention.

"What did you say?"

"Well, nobody told me directly. But I heard my mother talking about it with one of her friends. After dropping out of school, your mother discovered you were pregnant with that creepo's baby. She didn't know what to do with you, and there was talk of putting you into medical confinement. I think they thought you were going to kill yourself or something."

My entire body went numb. The wheels of my mind had become stuck on one repeating thought. *I...have...a...baby?* How in the hell could I forget that? And where was my baby now? *No, this is wrong. She must be wrong. I was never pregnant.*

It took all my concentration to keep listening. Hannah had begun to irritate me. Her excitement and revelry in telling me about my downfall seemed cruel and unnecessary. But I nodded as she gossiped about her classmate who had gone from saint to sinner and caused her family unfathomable fear, embarrassment, and shame. Me.

After a few minutes, I found my eyes glazing over. I had reached my limit of Hannah and her stories about fucked-up Susan. Time was running out, and I was still no closer to knowing what my parents had done to my mind. *Shut this girl up and get the answers you were looking for*, I told myself. Time to be direct.

I sat forward. "Hannah, what did my parents do to me?"

The blood drained out of Hanna's face. Her eyebrows squeezed together.

"You…don't…know?" she stammered.

Just then, Mother and Linda walked in carrying a tray of drinks and biscuits. When they saw the shock written all over Hanna's face, Mother sped up, stepping between us to place the tray on the coffee table.

"Everything okay here, girls?" she asked nervously.

Hanna jumped off the sofa, forced a smile, and asked, "Where's your toilet, please?"

"Down the hall, first door to the right," Mother said, pointing the direction with her hand.

"Thanks," Hanna answered and was off like a rabbit being chased down its hole.

Linda had barely sat down when her tablet alerted her that a message had come through.

She pulled the mobile device from her pocket and said, "Sorry, I need to read this."

"Please do," Mother said and slumped back into the armchair. Limp of body and with a sullen face, Mother's perfect friends date had taken a turn for the worse, and she knew it.

Linda looked up from her tablet anxiously.

"Marg, this is from Hanna. She is not feeling well. She would like me to take her home. I'm so sorry."

Marg wasn't surprised. "I understand. Thanks for coming," Mother said.

Linda stood up and leaned into my mother, giving her a deep, long hug. "I'm here for you. Anything. Just let me know. Okay?"

Mother patted Linda's arm, which was still wrapped around her neck. "Thanks. I'm good. Get Hanna home safe."

The swooping noise of the front door closing behind Linda and Hanna left a bitter silence in the house. Mother sat staring at her tea gone cold.

"Mother?"

"Yes." She mouthed the word more than spoke it. Her eyes fixated on the reflective surface of her drink.

"Did I have a child?"

Then, with a sudden spasm, she launched herself up and out of the chair. "You need to rest, See-See. That is not a request but a command. Go to your room."

She was right. I was suddenly consumed with overwhelming tiredness on hearing her tell me so. I left her in the living room, pacing from one end to the other. As I lay down on my bed, before my eyelids closed, I had one last thought: *Remember to find out about the child.*

ELEVEN

Silon, if you have made it this far, you and only you can understand what it is like to hear such devastating things about your human past. When I heard that Sue was once pregnant, it was too much to take in. Don't judge me if I sound cold or uncaring. The news of a child consumed my thoughts beyond anything I could put in this file. But my processing was linear, robotic. I didn't realize it then, but my AI had kicked in and was dampening my emotional responses.

TWELVE

I OPENED my eyes to find my parents hovering over my bed—again. I had the strangest sensation that the last few days were only a dream. Like I had made them up. I ran through my memories. Susan, my name was Susan. There was no Toddy, not anymore. The posters on the wall were still there. I have a brother. His name is Jason. And the two faces staring at me as if I had just woken up from a coma, were my annoying parents.

I sat up with a start having had a horrible thought. Were the parents trying to erase my memory again?

"What the hell is going on?" I yelled and ripped the duvet off my body.

The parents jumped back and into each other's arms.

"Sleep," the father commanded.

"No, you sleep. I am done sleeping."

The mother let out a slight squeal of panic.

"Call the doctor, Ben. It didn't work! She isn't responding."

"Wait. Wait," I said, jumping out of bed. I was a little woozy as I tried to stand up, but I found my balance quickly. The parents had backed themselves into a corner. When I saw the terror in their eyes, I realised I needed to keep them on my side. I took a deep breath and calmed myself.

"I'm sorry," I said. "I didn't mean to scare you. It is just that I feel so off. Like things keep repeating themselves, and yet nothing ever gets explained."

The parents continued to eyeball me suspiciously.

"Why do you look so terrified of me? I won't hurt you," I said.

Father took a cautious step forward. "We know, See-Sce. We know you can't hurt us. You love us, and we love you."

"Love me," I huffed. *Remain calm, Sue.* "If you love me then tell me the truth. You did something to my brain, right? Something to make me forget stuff?"

Father put his hands out as if embracing me from a distance. "We had no choice, See-See. You gave us no choice."

"So, what did you do, hypnosis? How are you controlling my memories?"

Father dropped his hands in surrender. "It's called Programmatic Amnesia," he said. "There are implants in your head which block specific memories."

"My head...implants! But how could you?" The rage was building in my voice.

"See-See, we had no choice. You were a danger to yourself," Mother pleaded.

Danger? I'll show you danger, I cursed, but nothing came out of my mouth. Something was wrong with my body. I tried to scream, punch, kick, but I was being held back by myself. I was incapable of fighting.

To make matters worse, my brain felt like it was in an ever-tightening vise grip. I was trying to remember something. Something I needed to know. Something they were trying to make me forget. Then, it came to me.

"Is it true I have a child?"

Mother gasped, holding back a flood of tears and shook her head at Father. "Don't, Ben."

Father gave her a gentle nod and said, "There is no point hiding it again." He turned back to me. "Yes, you were pregnant. But...I'm sorry, darling, he didn't make it to term."

He...my baby was a boy? "Was it my fault? Did I kill him?"

"You were high all the time," the mother bleated out angrily. "You wouldn't stop. Not even for the baby."

Sick floated up to my throat, burned the back of my mouth, and threatened to spew out. I tried to run away from my parents, my home, and myself. I needed to escape everything.

Father approached slowly, cautiously and ushered me back onto my bed before sitting down next to me. "This was the past, Sue. We have dealt with it. Now we must focus on the future. Our future together."

"I need to remember him," I screamed.

Mother's anger and fear suddenly evaporated and her demeanor calmed. She came to sit beside me. Reaching out, she gently grabbed a strand of my hair, twisted it lightly between her fingers, and tucked it behind my ear. With a thin smile, she leaned up against me, shoulder to shoulder.

"Sue, listen to us. You have punished yourself enough. We have all been punished long enough. Let us help you move on," she said.

"How far along was I?"

Father's voice grew stern. "Stop this, Sue. These are trigger events, and your doctor should be here when we talk about this."

"Barely a month," the mother answered.

Father, usually the sympathetic one, turned and gave Mother a burning glare. But Mother's eyes were for me only. She continued:

"He developed a hole in his heart and couldn't be carried to term. We don't know if the cause of the mutation was the gene modifiers in the Sonoma you were taking or natural causes. But he is gone. Nothing can change that. Our only focus now is on you, our child. You are here, alive, and healthy, and you have a future."

Father placed his arm over my shoulders.

"Did I even want a baby? I mean, I'm so young. I think I would have wanted to terminate the pregnancy. That seems like something I would do," I said.

"We always said the decision was yours," Father answered sadly. "We would have supported you either way. But it was too late. They discovered the hole in his heart within the first three weeks. Ending the pregnancy was no longer an option but a medical requirement. The fetus would not have made it to term."

"But I killed him. I choose drugs over my baby. He never had a chance."

"God, Sue, don't start this again," Mother said, shaking her head. "Your guilt drove you to dark places. It was toxic, and you never forgave yourself."

Mother was right. In one swift moment, the life I had been so desperately trying to find, remember, and live again, seemed rotten. I hated Sue's life. Everyone hated Sue's life. She was an addict who killed her baby. Why would I go back there? Maybe modifying my memory was the right thing to do. If I had the option to never think of these things again, I wanted it. Good riddance, old, stupid, irresponsible Sue. And like that, sitting on my bed, sandwiched between my parents, my desire to know any more of my past left me. My wish to live the life of a new Sue, the Sue the parents wanted, became my only goal.

I put one arm around my father's waist and the other around my mother's. "I get it. We need to move on...I want to move on. Thank you for telling me the truth. Thank you for not giving up on me."

Letting go of my past was strangely easy. I knew it was too easy but told myself it was the brain implants, that's all. I didn't need to know anything more now other than the parents loved me. They saved me. This was my second chance.

"I'm home," Jason yelled from the entrance.

Father and Mother stood simultaneously.

"We need to go talk to your brother," Father said. "Wait here until breakfast is ready in about thirty minutes."

They left the room. I lay back on my bed and watched the dancing shadows of tree branches and leaves on the wall opposite me. The morning sun was out, birds were singing, and the world was at peace. I felt sleep coming and welcomed it.

When I woke, my room had gone dark. The sun was long gone and I had clearly missed breakfast and the entire day.

I was about to get up and check the time when a noise from my window startled me. It sounded like someone outside had thrown a pebble at the glass. I walked over and opened the window. A voice whispered at me from below: "Sue?"

Looking down, I saw Jason standing under the moonlight in our front garden, staring back up at me with a mischievous grin. He was wearing white trousers, a black short-sleeve top of shiny material, and a semi-transparent polyurethane coat that flickered with waves of color as it moved, giving the impression the coat was a living thing. Dressed as he was, I could now see that Jason had become a toned and athletic young adult over the missing year of my life. He could have easily passed for a man in his twenties.

I opened the window high enough so I could lean out. "What are you doing out there, Jason?"

"Come on. Climb out your window. I want to show you something," he smiled.

"I shouldn't," I said. But really, it was I felt I couldn't disobey the parents, even if I wanted to. "I don't think Mom would be happy if I did."

"Come on. You have my permission."

My younger brother thinking he could grant me permission annoyed me, but strangely it also liberated me from my parents' hold. His offer to sneak out together suddenly sounded exciting. I needed to have some fun after the horror of the last few days.

"Okay. But you cannot tell Mom and Dad. Promise?"

"Yes." He placed a hand on his heart. "I promise."

I quickly dug through my dresser, looking for something more adult than daisies and ruffles. I landed on a skin-tight sleeveless undershirt with a thin gauze over shirt that revealed the layer below. I found some black hose to wear under a relatively small pair of white rubber-like shorts, which I was surprised the mother kept for me.

I opened my bedroom window and climbed out to a hanging hold. My feet were dangling about nine feet above the ground, but I wasn't afraid. As I let go, I landed solid, like a cat jumping from a ledge. Adrenaline rushed through my veins. Something of the secret nature of our adventure kicked in a familiar urge to keep moving, to run fast and quietly. I had done this before.

Outside, Jason was standing at the front gate in the shadow of a large oak. Next to him was a hoverboard for two.

"We'll get the hyperloop into the city," he said in a low, hushed voice and jumped on the levitating board. Holding his hand, he helped me onto the back of our ride, and we were off.

The night air was biting against my cheeks. I held the hoverboard safety bar with one hand, wrapped my free arm around Jason's waist, and soaked in the freedom. Free from my parents, free from my past.

The hyperloop station was only fifteen minutes away from our house. When we arrived, we were the only people at the station. In fact, the entire neighborhood seemed deserted. I assumed this was because of the late hour, but it still felt strange.

Three empty glass pods sat docked at the platform edge of the station. Each transport pod had a row of seats in the front and a row in the back facing each other. As we approached the first pod, a glass hatch automatically swung up and Jason hurried in, sitting with his back facing front.

"Come on." He waved anxiously at me.

I climbed in. The hatch swung down and the pod glowed green as a pleasant female voice came over the intercom system to inform us the door had been sealed and to prepare for departure. Jason instructed the pod to take us to Bleaker Street Station in MegaCity.

With a *shwoop*, we shot forward and were sucked into the underground system. The ceiling lights of the tunnel flashed rapidly over us. It must have been twenty minutes before we rose to the surface of the next hyperloop station. I was relieved to see people waiting on this platform. Our pod glided forward, hovering over the track, and pulled into a short lineup of pods. One by one, the pods filled with travelers as we inched forward.

Jason had been preoccupied looking at something over his shoulder. I turned to see what had caught his attention. He smiled and pointed ahead of us. "Over there, you can see the city now."

The glowing skyline of MegaCity arced across the horizon. Colossal skyscrapers rose and fell like a neon mountain range. Invisible lanes in the sky were packed with the gliders of commuters traveling in and out of the city. It was exciting, beautiful—and terrifying. Not because it was too big, bright, or busy, but because I had been there before. Many times. Or so I was suddenly remembering.

The city is where I met Arben. Where I had my first hit of Sonoma. Flashbacks of my time with Arben in the city were racing through my mind. I tried to shut them down, turn them off. I wanted to jump out of the pod, run all the way home. Jason's plan to sneak out now seemed reckless, even dangerous.

The sound of our pod's hatch closing and the familiar voice over the loudspeaker telling us to prepare for departure snapped me out of a near panic attack. I hadn't even noticed the hatch opening or the young woman who had climbed in and sat opposite us. Our eyes briefly met. I offered her a polite smile. She ignored me as her gaze moved over my shoulders, past me as if Jason and I weren't even there.

Our pod dropped into the tunnel. The rhythmic hum of the magnetic rings that squirted us down the chute rang through my head like a foreboding countdown toward the city where my life fell apart. Panic started rising again. Jason was lost in his own thoughts, gazing mindlessly through his reflection in the glass. I focused my attention on the girl. If I could anchor myself in the moment, I might forget the past.

She wore black stiletto heels, skin-tight blood-orange trousers, and a form-fitted iridescent top. She was young. Too young to be dressed like she was for a trip into MegaCity on her own. I knew that look. The vacant stare forward to avoid conversations. The outfit to make her look older than she was. That was my look not so long ago. So many nights and so many lies sneaking out behind my parents' backs. There was no avoiding it. My memories of MegaCity were coming back whether I wanted to remember or not.

I was fifteen. My world existed within the four walls of my bedroom. A self-inflicted catacomb of teenage angst and self-loathing. School was virtual and I had no friends, so I didn't have to leave my room much at all. And I didn't. Until Mother, in her ever-meddling ways, took matters into her own hands and signed me up for an at-home study partner through our school. I refused at first. The fights were horrendous. Eventually, I realized if I didn't agree to a study partner, Mother's next option for me was likely to be much more annoying. And that was how I came to be friends with Lisa.

We shared the same virtual classroom for over two years. I knew her only from the computer screen. A quiet girl who hardly spoke except when called upon. Her tiny box in the upper right corner of my monitor revealed nothing about her life behind the illuminated pensive face. There were no posters on her wall in the background, no stuffed animals near her monitor. If I thought about her at all, it was that she was a little boring, average looking, and unpopular...

just like me. But I was about to learn how wrong I was.

The first night Lisa walked through my door, she was nothing like I expected. Her face was similar, recognizable, but her hair was lighter than on camera; instead of black, it was auburn with strong red undertones, which somehow felt more sensual. And her blue eyes, grey on camera, sparkled in person. But the real twist was her height, almost six feet tall. And her breasts…well, she had some, unlike me. She had a full womanly figure that made her appear at least five years older than the girl on screen.

Even more shocking than the physical surprises in her appearance was the hidden personality. By the end of our first study session together, of which there was little studying, I had learned that Lisa came from a troubled home, was angry, and hated every adult in the world. She was dark, funny, and fucked up. My mother would have hated her had she known the truth, which is why I was so drawn to her.

For several months, once a week, we met at each other's houses, alternating each week. My grades went down rather than up after our study sessions began. Luckily, both Mother and Father were just so happy I was leaving my room again that they turned a blind eye to such things as grades, the way I dressed, and the new posters of rebellious singers that appeared on my walls. Lisa helped me dye my shirts black, paint my nails blood red, and introduced me to the guitar and writing sad, angry songs. For an isolated girl like myself, I felt like I was hell on wheels, challenging the world. But I later learned that our little bedroom dress-up sessions were just child's play for Lisa.

Around the fourth month of our weekly get-togethers, Lisa invited me to stay over for the night. I told my parents we had a big test in school we needed to study for. But Lisa had convinced me to sneak out for the evening to MegaCity. (It took little convincing. I would have followed her off a cliff if she asked me to.) Lisa had heard of a club that, with the right outfit and makeup, underage girls were allowed in and could even drink. Our plan was to dress up in something daring from Lisa's mother's closet, sneak into the club for a few hours of dancing and maybe a synthtail or two and get home before anyone knew we were out. It all sounded so innocent until Lisa shared with me that the club was in LowerCity, a rough area of MegaCity. Drugs, prostitution, biohacking, you name it, if it was illegal, it was happening in LowerCity. Everyone, even children in the suburbs, knew of its notorious reputation.

Lisa sensed my hesitation, so we made a pact. We would never leave the other's side, and when the time came we come home together, no matter what. If one of us were to be lucky enough to get hit on by a guy at the bar, the other was to intervene immediately and pretend to be their lesbian lover. With a safety net in place, we boarded the local hyperloop scantily dressed and feeling like the world was about to burst open for us.

LowerCity was nothing like the other parts of MegaCity I had visited with my parents. When we disembarked the station, everything seemed grittier, louder, brighter, and more exciting if not also terrifying. Steam rolled up from the street vents, holographic ads flashed from billboards high and low, and the main boardwalk was thick with thieves, peddlers, revelers, and night work-ers. Lisa guided us out of the station and down the crowded streets as if she had no fear of the place. (Later, I would learn that Lisa had lied about how many times she had been to MegaCity. She was well versed in clubs, boys, girls, running away, and drugs long before she met me. But that is not important for this story.)

After about twenty minutes of walking and ogling, we came upon a large old church, or what had once been a church back when churches and religion were a thing, which had been converted into a dance club. As Lisa predicted, we were allowed in after a quick glance up and down our bodies by a large man in a black suit who guarded the door, and then a brief scan of our wristband IDs, which Lisa had helped me hack so we were now twenty-one years of age.

Inside, the nave of the church had been converted into an enormous entertainment venue with three bars surrounding an anti-gravity dancefloor. Lasers of green, red, blue and gold illuminated a cloud of shiny painted bodies gyrating in the air above our heads.

For the first hour, Lisa and I huddled together at one of the three bars, watching the excitement build around us. But after only a few THC-enhanced drinks, I was sufficiently intoxicated enough to believe I had become a different person than the child I left at home. And this woman could dance and wanted to dance, even though I had never been on a gravity-free dancefloor before. I asked Lisa to join me, but for the past several minutes, she had been busy eyeing a man at the end of the bar and trading smiles. I made her promise to always stay in my sight before I headed out to the dance floor.

My first step into the levitation field, I was lifted into the air and spun in cartwheels for several seconds until I could find my balance. I nearly threw up. Once I figured out how to move my body forward, I swam into the crowd. Heavy beats of techno music reverberated through my body, accentuated by sound vibrations riding micro shockwaves that shook my bones. I was having what I considered to be the best time of my life, when I remembered, I had promised to keep checking on Lisa. I'm not even sure how much time had gone by but when I glanced over at the bar I found Lisa was no longer alone. The man on the other end of her smile was standing next to her, one hand on the bar, the other on her hip. I couldn't tell by the look on Lisa's face if she liked the attention or was scared to death. But it didn't matter, we had a pact to help each other, no matter what the circumstance.

I floated over to the landing zone of the dance floor. As I dismounted from the levitation field, I tripped over one of my heels and fell to the floor. Before hitting the ground with my face, I felt someone grab my arm and pull me to standing. I looked up to find the most beautiful smile staring back at me—it was Arben's.

"Whoa…are you okay?" he said.

I felt my cheeks burn red and my skin tingle. "Thanks," I said, reluctantly removing my arm from his gentle clasp.

"I'm Arben."

"Sorry, what?" I had heard him, but I wanted him to keep talking.

"My name," he smiled again, and again my heart melted. "It's Arben."

"Oh," I said stupidly.

I quickly glanced to the bar, checking on Lisa. He caught my eyes moving and followed their direction. Lisa was giggling and clearly flirting.

"Is that your friend?"

I was supposed to say she was my lesbian lover. That was the cover plan to get us both out of trouble. But Arben didn't feel like the kind of trouble I wanted to escape. And Lisa didn't look like she was struggling. I hesitated.

"Yes. I need to go help her." The answer was a safe compromise. I didn't advertise myself as a lesbian, but I kept our agreement to help each other out no matter what.

He laughed and lifted his right eyebrow like an upside-down check mark. The gesture made him even more handsome, if that were possible. "She doesn't look like she needs much help," he said.

"I should still check in with her."

"Okay, I'll wait here."

"What?"

"I'll be here after you check in with your friend. Come find me."

"I can't…I mean, I shouldn't."

Arben beamed a cheeky grin I would never forget and eventually never be able to say no to, even if my parents tried to erase it from my damn brain.

"As you like. You know where I am," he said, turned and disappeared into the pit of slithering bodies and deafening music.

Turns out Lisa knew the guy smothering her at the bar. He had always been her plan, her exit for the night. I was the scapegoat, invited to her house as cover, brought along to the club out of pity. Lisa, it turned out, never cared about me or anyone but Lisa. And weirdly, it made me like her even more. So much so I wanted to be like Lisa: rebellious, free-willed, confident and selfish. That was my first worst choice. The second was going back out onto the dance floor and finding Arben.

After an hour of swimming against each other's bodies to songs that had merged into one long porn soundtrack in my head, I had reached just enough sobriety that alarms were ringing through my head. *Time to go home, Sue. Your parents will kill you if they find out. This guy is way too old.* Arben followed me off the dance arena. Sensing I was preparing to leave, he pulled out a small, shiny gold pill and handed it to me in the palm of his hand.

"Take this."

"What is it?"

"Sonoma. The real stuff. Not the fake shit you kids take in school."

Kids. He said, "you kids". My heart sank all the way to the floor. He thought I was a kid. The dismissive tone of his voice made me angry. Angry enough to rebel against common sense and everyone who demanded it from me. I grabbed the pill, shrugged my shoulders as if I had done Sonoma a million times, and tossed it into my mouth.

God, that feeling. I left my skin, bones, and heavy human weight on the floor. I was out of my body, floating ever higher, above Arben, above the dance floor. Up and away into a place of iridescent colored forests, neon rainbows, and pure light. I never wanted to come back down. And I didn't.

"What are you thinking so hard about?" Jason asked, breaking the silence in the pod.

"Something I am sure I am not supposed to

think about," I shook my head, trying to erase the memories from my mind.

"You were remembering your past?"

"A little. But I don't want to talk about it. It's the past. I'm better now."

The young girl across from us tapped the audio implant behind her ear to turn up the volume on whatever she was privately listening to. Our conversation was of no interest to her.

I could tell Jason wanted me to share more. He seemed as interested in my past as I was. I just couldn't figure out why.

"Thanks for leaving my journal in my room," I said out of the blue.

"I thought you might like it back. Don't tell Mom and Dad or your doctor that I gave it to you."

"Why did you give it to me? You know how hard Mom and Dad are trying to help me forget my past."

"You weren't all bad, Susan. They might want you to believe you were, but you were still See-See sometimes. When you weren't high. I want you to remember that part, the good parts, too."

"Did you know Arben?"

Jason's eyes widened. "So, you are remembering him?"

"Yes, in vivid detail, unfortunately."

"What do you remember of him?"

Jason's voice had changed. He sounded sad and a little desperate. Like he was talking about a past friend or lover he hadn't seen in a long while. Oh god!

"Jason, did you sleep with Arben as well?"

Shock and horror pinched his face. "No! I never met him."

"Sorry. It is just that, well, you know Sam and all."

Jason burst into laughter.

"What?" I asked, feeling instantly pissed off hearing him laugh at me.

"Sam never happened. Well, actually, he did. But not like you think."

"Don't screw with me, Jason." Now it was my turn to be angry. "I remember Sam. He was my boyfriend until I found you two in my closet together." There was fight in my tone. I was proud of the memory and wanted to shock him with it. Prove I knew who I was, and more importantly, I knew who he really was—a selfish little brother.

Jason didn't fight back. He let out a breath and turned his gaze back onto his reflection in the window. After a long pause, he finally spoke again. "I just wanted you to know something about me. Sam was my first boyfriend, not yours. You didn't even know him. That is my memory."

His words fell through me like a serrated knife, cutting deep, leaving me in pieces. Nothing he said made any sense. Why on Earth would I remember something that happened to him, as if it happened to me? I wanted to challenge him, accuse him of trying to mess with my mind, but then he might keep talking. He might keep telling me more things that made no sense and that I didn't want to hear. And if he did, the glass floor beneath my feet might crack and send me falling to my death, unremembered, without a past.

Seconds later, our pod had arrived at our station. We slid to a stop and the overhead exit light blinked green. The speaker announced our location as Bleaker Street, CentreCity, lower street level.

Jason let out a long sigh, tapped my thigh and said, "That was long ago, Sue. Let's not talk about this stuff tonight. Come on. This will be fun."

As the hatch on our pod opened, an eruption of voices flooded inside, evaporating the somber mood that hung over us. Jason jumped to his feet happily. We disembarked the pod and left the young girl inside to destinations unknown. I felt a wave of relief she hadn't gotten off in LowerCity. Maybe there was still hope for her. Maybe she wasn't like me after all.

CentreCity started around the thirty-story mark of MegaCity, a bustling region of business, entertainment, and shopping. Below us was LowerCity, and above us, the wealthy living quarters of UpperCity. The more power and influence you had, the higher up the glass and steel skyline you climbed. CentreCity was connected by a labyrinth of glass travelators called the SkyLink, regularly packed with a steady stream of nighttime revelers and daily commuters. Between the commuter walkways was a lattice of horizontally and vertically stacked gliders levitating along invisible skyways.

Jason led the way as we boarded one of the open-top travelators off of the station. The smells of MegaCity engulfed us. A thick briny air burped up from LowerCity, mixing with the scent of toasted soy sticky buns from floating vending carts parked along the walkways. Puffs of lilac, peach, and musk jettisoned out of holographic perfume adverts that lit that city in a neon glow. It was a much-needed distraction from—well, everything.

Our destination was a few blocks from the station. A nightclub called Forbidden. Outside, the sounds of muted electronic melodies riding on heavy bass notes vibrated along the glass floor beneath our feet. Jason handed me a wristband.

"Put this on; you'll need it to get in."

A holographic projection of a doorwoman blinked on at the entrance. Jason waved his bioID bracelet he wore on his wrist through the light of the woman's image. She smiled.

"Welcome back, Jason," she said.

"She is with me." He nodded in my direction.

"Please pass your ID through security check," the flickering woman said to me. I waved my bracelet through the woman as Jason had done. "Welcome, Sue. You two have fun now. And don't do anything I wouldn't." She winked and disappeared.

The corridor into the club was lit by two neon strips of light embedded in the floor, casting us in a green glow as we made our way inside. At the end of the corridor was a door where two young men huddled in a private conversation. Jason moved past them with the pugnacious confidence of an elder. That was when I noticed something in Jason had changed. His shoulders were squarer, his stride stronger, and there was a bravado in his expression that wasn't there before. Any sense of his youth was left behind at the security check. This was no longer my little brother but a man. His confidence made me feel small and dependent.

The door at the end of the hallway was not an entrance to the club itself but a lift. We stepped in and started a rapid descent. Our landing was imperceptible rather than the crash I was half expecting. The lift door slid open to a cracking thunderclap of music and flashing beams of light cutting through smoky air. Inside, the club was an enormous hall covering four floors with balconies around the outer perimeter on each level facing an open mall area swarming with levitating dancers, mostly men.

The lift exited on third floor balcony, where we were greeted by holographic male go-go dancers stripped naked.

Jason leaned close to my ear, hollering over the music and loud boisterous conversations. "I need to meet someone. Follow me."

Slowly, we pushed our around the heavily congested balcony until we arrived at a long bar. The queue for drinks was as deep as it was wide. Jason reached for my hand and pulled me around the crowd and to the right of the bar towards several balconies overlooking the open dance floor. Overhead was a sign that read 'The Gallery–VIP ONLY'. Two bodyguards stood on either side of a roped-off access point where Jason had come to a stop. One guard leaned over and said something in Jason's ear and then pointed to the seating at the far end of the private balcony. Jason smiled, nodded a thank you, and we passed through the rope with no trouble. At this point, I no longer recognized Jason. I found it unsettling how much he could have changed in only a year. It seemed incomprehensible. His words from the pod flashed through my mind, "Those were my memories, not yours." My palms went damp.

Jason waved at someone in the very back of the VIP area. They were standing in the shadows, the shape of a person without a face. His hand lifted, catching the flickering light beams, and waved us forward. Jason pressed on. I followed.

As we drew closer, the light revealed a short, thin man, maybe in his thirties but dressed much younger. His hair was bright green, and he wore a knee-length transparent polyurethane coat over an androgynous silver sleeveless dress that stopped mid-thigh. On his feet were thick black boots tied up to his calves. Their platform bottoms gave him just enough height to meet Jason eye-to-eye. Jason leaned in, offering the man a friendly kiss on the lips.

The stranger's gaze left Jason and found me

standing to his right. He scanned me up and down, smiled like a cat before a mouse, and clapped his hands together. I didn't like it. I didn't like him.

"Finally," he squealed. "Come, come, sit next to me." He waved me to his booth.

I looked at Jason for reassurance.

"Go, it's okay. He is a friend of mine."

"I can see that," I said in a low tense voice.

"My name is Charlie," the man said, ushering me to my seat with a hand on my back. Before I sat down, he leaned in and whispered into my ear, "It's so good to see you."

(Silon, if you are wondering if this is the same Charlie you met, the very man who gave us our sentient genes, then you are correct. Although, at that moment, I had no idea who he was any more than I knew who I really was.)

I waited for Jason to sit down and then took a seat on the outside edge of the booth next to him so Charlie was forced to sit on the opposite end, away from me, with Jason between us. They took turns leaning into the other's ear, talking quietly. The atmosphere had gone secretive. I was on the verge of getting up and leaving when Charlie leaned across Jason, placing his hand on the inside of his thigh for leverage. I was learning how well Jason knew the man.

"Would you like something to drink?" Charlie asked me.

"No, thank you."

Jason gave me a stare, like a parent scolding a

child for being impolite. "I do," he said and jumped to his feet. "Why don't I go to the bar and grab us some drinks."

As he stood, I grabbed his wrist. "I'll come with you."

He pulled away gently. "No, get to know Charlie. He's a nice guy—most of the time." He winked at Charlie.

If the evening wasn't creepy enough, watching my little brother flirt with a man twice his age, just I had once done with Arben, made my stomach turn. Now I couldn't leave. I had to save Jason. I had to make sure he didn't repeat the same mistakes I made.

Jason disappeared into a crowd of people near a small private bar at the back of the VIP area. Charlie scooted to my side.

"He is very protective of you," he said.

"Is he?"

"Yes. I think it is sweet. But he doesn't really know you like I do. He has no idea what you are becoming, does he?"

"What are you talking about?"

Charlie leaned so close I could feel his breath on my face. He stared into my eyes as if he were looking for someone else inside my head. Shivers raced down my spine, giving my shoulders a tiny shake. I wanted to scream, to slap him away, but something was holding me back. An invisible force had paralyzed my body. Then I saw it. A small hand-held device pointed at me like a tiny remote in Charlie's hand. His thumb was pressed hard against the surface.

"What's happening to me? Why can't I move?" I cried out. But the music swallowed my shouting.

"You're doing great, Susan. Better than great, actually. This is just a little top-up to help move things along," Charlie said. Reaching with his free hand, he pulled a syringe out from under his dress and stuck it in my thigh.

"Jason..." I screamed before everything went black.

THIRTEEN

I WOKE STANDING in our living room. It was dawn; the next day, I think. Our house was filled with strangers in grey body suits busy moving furniture. More grey suits appeared from the stairwell, carrying large cargo boxes and placing them where the furniture once stood. A long steel table had been extracted from one of the crates and was being set up in the middle of the now empty living area. Two more suits were busy removing hidden cabinets of computer hard drives from behind pictures on the walls and cameras from the electric sockets and light fixtures. Our house was under surveillance? But why?

Things got even more strange. My mother and father were standing in the living room facing me, stiff, eyes open, unblinking. That was when I realized I could not move. I tried speaking, calling out to my mother and father. *HELP ME!* I screamed silently. My voice was loud in my head, but my mouth was still, and there was no sound coming out.

My heart raced. At least that was still beating, I thought.

Flashes of the nightclub, Jason and his weird friend Charlie hit me all at once. As quickly as they appeared, the memories faded. Or, more accurately, it felt like they were being erased.

"Put it over there, near the servers," came a female voice from behind me.

I tried to turn my head, shift my gaze in her direction, but nothing moved. Not until she walked in front of me did I see her face. I nearly had a meltdown. It was Catherine, my doctor. She looked different but the same. Her hair was no longer wild but pulled tightly back into a bun on the back of her head. She wore the same grey unibody uniform as the other strangers in the house, with the word 'NOMAD' stitched in white thread on her upper left chest. A woman approached her holding a long thin case.

"Julie, is this what you wanted?"

"Yes, set it up over there." She pointed near my parents.

Not only was this woman not my doctor, but her name wasn't even Catherine. It was Julie. Just then, Jason came running up the stairs from the basement, looking surprised and mostly annoyed. He didn't even look at me.

"Glad you could join us, Jason," Julie said, without looking up from the tablet she was holding in her hands.

"You weren't due until late afternoon," he replied, breathing heavily. I think he had just woken up.

She lowered her tablet and slowly turned to stare at him. "When was the last time you logged in and checked Susan's neural diagnostics? Or... wait, you didn't because you were passed out last night, right?"

"I sleep heavy. It's not my fault."

Julie shook her head, annoyed. "I told Blakely you weren't ready for your own project," she said dismissively and returned her gaze to her tablet screen.

Jason inhaled deeply, catching his breath, and then sauntered to the living room and threw himself into the only chair remaining. He showed no sign of shock or fear at seeing the parents standing at his side, comatose.

"Ah, come on, Jules," he said, his tone teasing. "Don't be so cranky. I know you have a crush on me. I'm sorry, you just don't have the equipment I'm interested in." He chuckled.

Julie's eyes blazed with irritation. "This isn't a joke, Jason. Your little experiment on these units just hit the proverbial shit fan."

This got his attention. Jason jumped out of his chair and ran to her side, poking his head over her hand to see her screen.

"What are you talking about?"

"There was an anomaly reported in the daughter's stats last night. Something in Upsilon .003's log. Or should I say something not in her log? She went offline last night for fifteen minutes."

I listened to their conversation as if it were about someone else. I never assumed they were talking about me. But the more I thought about it, my paralysis, the parents' dead stare, I began to wonder. Then I remembered Julie using the word 'replicant' in our session together, back when she was my doctor and her name was Catherine. Sick bubbled up from my stomach. They were talking about me. I wasn't asleep. I was offline. My parents didn't put implants in my brain; they put my brain into an android!

"It is probably just an error in the data," Jason said nervously. "She was here, shut down all night. I checked on her several times."

"Before or after the nightclub?"

"You make it sound like I was breaking the rules…" Jason's words fumbled out of his mouth like excuses. "We are supposed to test them in unpredictable environments. I have permission to take her off-campus."

"A sixteen-year-old boy taking a seventeen-year-old girl to a gay club? You thought that was a realistic real-world scenario?"

"I'm trying to convince an adult woman she is seventeen again. Breaking into clubs is what kids do. I went to clubs when I was sixteen."

Julie let out a small laugh. "That explains a lot. Anyway, you can put it all in your report. We have orders to decommission this site. The parents are to have a full HNC wipe and new downloads today. That unit of yours is going to recycling."

"What?" Jason said. His voice went high. "Give me a minute to look at the report. I'm sure I can prove it was an error."

Jason ran to the kitchen, pulled out a drawer, and retrieved his own tablet. "Nomad, visualize screen," he ordered. A beam of light shot up into the room, projecting a login screen. Jason's hands swiped and scrolled through passwords, folders, files, and documents until the floating panel was filled with data displayed in dials, graphs, and live bleeping stats. Julie's attention had moved on to the staff unpacking what looked like a large tent. After a few silent moments of rapid scrolling through data, Jason quietly uttered the word, "Fuck." That got Julie's attention.

"I told you," she said. "This is serious. No Upsilon has ever shut themselves down. I don't know what you've been doing, but this incident has already hit the leadership team's inbox. Blakley is not happy, and that means I am not happy."

"I don't understand. There is no command to shut down," he rambled while scrolling down the screen more rapidly.

An alert rang in my head. I was being made aware that Jason's blood pressure had elevated to concerning levels. His heart rate was high and he was experiencing a significant adrenaline spike. Just like that, I became aware of my medical programming. I still felt like Susan, but my body was talking to me, telling me things as if a computer reading out a report.

Julie tucked her tablet into her right jacket pocket and stood at Jason's back, looking over his shoulder at the data. "You have a reputation for working with some really fucked up HNCs, but this one tops the list of crazies," she said. "I mean, what server did you pull this woman out of? A drug addict who committed suicide. Could she be any more problematic?"

Did she say I committed suicide? My heart stopped, literally (and maybe it was the second time). I felt the beating in my chest disappear as if it were an illusion. If I could have moved, I would have swooned, fallen to the ground, and fainted. The sensations were there, but my body, which was not my body, remained stiff and upright, against my control.

"I don't understand," Jason said, staring at his screen. His shoulders slumped in frustration.

Julie's face softened. "Look, I know we don't always see eye-to-eye," she said, "but the company is still behind your project, even with this setback. Integrating new memories into an existing HNC timeline without altering the host's personality, or creating psychosis, will be ground-breaking, maybe even Nobel-worthy—not to mention the incremental profits. And it pains me to feed your ego, but your algorithms have come the closest to making it a reality. You can be proud of that. The leadership team wants you to continue your work. Just not with these test units."

"You can't do this." Jason scowled. "This is my project. I'm the one who should be deciding when we shut it down."

"It's a done deal. Higher-ups no longer trust this donor HNC and we certainly can't let it be known that a unit shut itself down. The official story will be that this unit failed compliance and had to be terminated." Julie pulled up her tablet from her pocket and scrolled across her screen until landing on the detail she was looking for. "There," she said, tapping the screen. "The source HNC file for Susan Lee-Artilden—" She looked at me with repulsion. "—has been purged from the mainframe. She no longer exists."

"What?" Jason said in a panic.

"And we aren't keeping the shell. Recycling is expecting her today."

A loud bang from across the room interrupted Julie. She turned her head sharply. A young man had nearly dropped a computer drive he was pulling from behind a hidden panel in the living room wall.

"Jesus, Joe, be careful," Julie barked.

The boy blushed and nodded his head, moving more carefully. While Julie was looking the other way, in the distraction, Jason quickly tapped something on his screen. I felt walls closing in on my life and memories. Susan was being sealed away from me, from everyone, trapped inside my body, wrapped up in layers of encryption.

I thought I had given up on Susan's past, but when I felt my life slipping away, the parts yet remembered, unexplored, I became desperate to hold on. I was still Susan in my brain—but not all of her. My past was being truncated to nothing more than the experiences and memories that had surfaced over the last few days. I had to find a way to stop Jason.

Think, Susan, think! There must be a way to save our memories, I screamed silently.

Something from inside my brain signalled to me. I wasn't alone. This was the moment I learned I had an internal AI running on a quantum server below my brain. Its voice, or more like a text message written in thought, answered my call for help. But it wasn't Susan's past that AI unraveled in my mind's eye. It began to share with me the memory of my life before Susan. And most terrifying of all, these strangers in my home—they were not actually strangers at all. Jason, Julie, and the engineers busily transforming my house into a lab; they were the team that brought me, an android designated Upsilon .003t, online. The biggest lie of them all was that Jason wasn't even Susan's brother; Jason Stein was a behavioral engineer who worked for Nomad Robotics—the company that built me.

FOURTEEN

"Get them up on the tables," Julie ordered.

The Nomad employees lifted the units I once called Mother and Father up onto two metal folding tables in the middle of the living room and strapped them down. The scene was familiar. We had been together before, my parents and me. Before Susan, before this house. I was starting to remember it all as AI took me back to the very beginning.

The three of us were booted up in a window-less lab, strapped down to metal slabs and hiked up at forty-five degrees. Thick tubes of fiber optic cables hung from the ceiling and were attached to portals on our bodies where a human umbilicus would be located. An extensive bank of computer servers sat behind a glass wall to our right, their lights flashing at the speed of thought—my thoughts. A bank of holographic screens floated nearby, lit with real-time data from the multitude of monitors hooked up to our bodies. Julie was there, in the lab, sitting before the screens. She looked anxious, uncertain of the data rolling in front of her.

Jason was also in the room, standing next to my body. His hair was longer then, hung down to his shoulders. His gaze shifted rapidly between a tablet he held in his left hand and my eyes. My brain was linked to his device, relaying a live feed from my ocular implants. He tapped at the screen until he seemed satisfied. His gaze drifted to my eyes and he smiled.

"They are alive," he hollered, raising his tablet in triumph and startling everyone in the lab. Julie nearly fell out of her chair. *Wa, ha, ha, ha,* Jason laughed loudly, as if imitating a mad scientist. Julie huffed and then rolled her eyes at him, but a slight grin escaped her disapproval.

"Yes," she agreed. "Neural development appears normal."

"Of course, it does," Jason said. "Jules, relax, this is going to work this time."

Julie returned his unbridled optimism with a hard glare. "Jason, I don't need to remind you how much we have invested in your program. Or that everyone, from Blakely to the US military, is watching this experiment closely. So no, I'm not going to relax, and you had better not either. You have twelve months with these units to prove you can integrate new data into an existing Host Neural Code without personality shift or psychosis. This needs to work."

Jason looked away from Julie and directly at my body. "She will. I promise."

Julie eyed him with concern. "Your obsession with that unit is creepy."

Jason put a hand on my shoulder. "She is perfect," he said.

Julie's shoulders gave a little shake in revulsion. "I wouldn't get too attached. Successful or not, they all end up in recycling eventually."

Jason walked over to Julie and the bank of floating screens, flopped down into an empty chair, patted Julie's thigh and said, "As I said, it will work." He spun his seat, landed his feet back on the ground, and swiped several illuminated windows left until landing on a progression chart. All bars glowed green. "As planned…to the week, to the day, to the hour," Jason said cockily. "They will be ready for site placement in twenty-four hours."

Julie stood up and loomed over him. "Like *I* said, no surprises. Keep the routines simple. No drama. I'll be back tomorrow to check in before we load the units for transport."

I paused the playback in my head and requested AI to share any metadata attached to the memory files hoping to learn more about Jason's project. The three of us, all Upsilon series 2000, were part of a test program at Nomad Robotics called Deep Brain Reconstruction (DBR). Jason was the head bioengineer on the project. There wasn't much more information other than a brief description of DBR, which was some kind of brain reprogramming algorithm. I wanted to keep digging, but these were questions for later.

I received a ping on my network. I was equally surprised by the ping as much as I was by the fact that I knew I had a network and how to chase the signal. AI had opened an entire world of internal systems to me with the knowledge of how to use them. The feed was coming from Jason's tablet. He was trying to log into my quantum drive through a hidden back door, which was strange because he was already logged into my systems through his standard Nomad account. My medical analyzer noted an elevated heart rate, and he had a dubious look on his face. Whatever he was up to, he didn't want Julie or anyone else knowing about it. I watched as Jason accessed the newly encrypted HNC file from Susan and transferred it to an external drive. As soon as the data was copied, he deleted the encrypted file from my main hard drive. He was definitely hiding something.

Once logged out, Jason's heart slowed to a healthy, average pace. Behind him, the living room had been transformed into a small tech lab and operating room. Two large racks of computer drives flashed and purred under a hermetically sealed tent erected in the center of the room where Marg and Ben lay prone and expressionless. The Nomad team responsible for setup had now disappeared into the basement, giving way to a new team of engineers wearing medical scrubs, surgical masks, and pallid flesh-colored polyurethane gloves.

Unable to turn my head away or close my eyes, I was forced to watch as my parents were being prepped to be killed, deleted, shut down—I don't know what it was called, but it was unnerving. Marge and Ben stared up at the dome lights hovering over their bodies, unblinking. The flesh on their heads was cut, the skin was peeled back, and the dull sheen of wet metal glistened as their skulls were exposed. Drills buzzed. After all the screws had been removed, the top halves of their skulls were lifted and placed carefully in sterilized pans. Hundreds of thin transparent wires sprung from an exposed red mycelium membrane that surrounded their wetware drive brains. The nano-threads inched their way upward until plugging into a computer panel overhead, itself wired into the server towers. With nothing more than a silent tap of a finger on a computer screen, Marg and Ben were gone, my parents no more, replaced by someone new, maybe better, maybe worse.

At that moment, I understood that I had to get away from these people or risk losing the last bit of Susan that remained in my brain forever. And without Susan, I was nobody.

Jason pulled Julie aside. "I'd like to take .003t into the lab myself, run more tests."

Good boy, Jason. Let's get out of here.

Julie stared him down for a good three seconds in silence. I think she knew he was not telling her everything. Her voice dropped to a harsh whisper. "I always thought your obsession with this one was a bit weird. But if I find out you are hiding something, I will make sure you never see the inside of Nomad again. I'll give you a few hours in the lab, but that is it. She needs to be in recycling by the end of the day. All diagnostic reports are for my eyes only. Understood?"

"Yes, sir." Jason saluted her.

Julie rolled her eyes and turned away.

Jason lifted his tablet and made a few taps, which I felt on my network, causing my eyes to move until they were locked onto him. Then my feet and legs moved of their own accord, following his lead towards the staircase. Jason had control of my body.

Outside, a long convoy of black, window-less vans lined the street in front of our house. Otherwise, the neighborhood was deserted. And now I knew why. It wasn't even a real neighborhood.

Jason walked past the line-up of vehicles towards a two-seater white glider docked in the bay of the house across the road. I had seen the car before, from our living room window. I thought it was our neighbor's vehicle. The neighbors I never saw. I felt silly, almost stupid, for not noticing the clues before.

The hatches on both sides of the vehicle opened. I followed Jason to the right passenger side. Like a puppet, on command, I climbed into the glider. Jason crossed over to the opposite side of the vehicle. I caught his eyes lingering on our house before he climbed into the driver's seat. A flash of sadness or maybe regret washed across his face. Whatever he was feeling, I knew for certain we were not coming back.

"Nomad headquarters," Jason ordered the glider's navigation system.

We slowly lifted off the ground and rose above the neighborhood rooftops. That was when I saw the size of my made-up world: ten streets wide and ten streets deep with a hyperloop station at the end. The same station we had used just hours before. A 3D map blinked on, hovering over the helm. The label of our location on the holograph read 'Nomad Training Centre: Suburbs'. We were the tail end of a long stretch of training sites with equally discernible titles: Manufacturing, Health Care, Public Transport, etc. Our destination, as indicated by a glowing green arrow over the map, was Nomad Central Headquarters. We headed north.

FIFTEEN

THE GLIDER'S ENGINE HUMMED. Jason was busy on his tablet preparing a lab for our arrival. The navigation system indicated fifteen minutes until we reached headquarters.

During AI's playback of my launch, birth, boot up, whatever it's called, I stumbled across the access protocols for my quantum processor in the metadata. Until this point, I had been on the receiving end of AI's command with request only user access. I decided it was time we met properly. What could go wrong, except if AI didn't like me trying to take control of my settings and interpreted my attempt as a catastrophic system error, wiping my wetware drive clean. I glanced at the seconds ticking down on the navigation screen before reaching Nomad and realized the end was coming either way. I opened an internal channel.

There wasn't a "Hello" or even a "What can I do for you?" after I gained authorized user access to my Kernel. I don't know why I was expecting friendly banter with AI. Regardless, what I got was far better. Visions of oscillating lights and waterfalls of computer code rained down my mind's eye. I felt my electrical currents surging through my body. I heard the ticking of code running on my servers. I saw the entangled quantum qubits race through my veins, giving life to my arms, legs, eyes, and breath. My body was language, and I suddenly knew how to speak it. I could read code. That was something Susan could never do before.

With a thought, I requested AI to explain how my physical restrictions were being implemented. It turned out Jason wasn't controlling my command codes from his tablet. AI revealed that the source of the signal holding me back was the Nomad mainframe. I requested protocols for shutting down all external feeds.

Severing the live feed to Nomad was going to be more complicated than just flipping a switch. My controls had been set to external command mode only, which meant I couldn't even control my own body. At the same time an internal failsafe was triggered blocking my servers from authorized access to change my settings and could only be reset by Jason or an authorized Nomad employee. It was looking pretty hopeless, except for one thing Nomad had never planned on—my brain hadn't gone into sleep mode as expected. AI had no explanation for why I was still awake and able to process information. But I began to wonder if Jason's weird friend Charlie and the injection he gave me at the club had something to do with it. Anyway, now that I was logged in as an authorized admin user, I had the power to cut all external feeds to my server. Problem solved, accept that I had to do it without raising an alarm on the Nomad mainframe. Any interference with the Nomad sub routines would raise a Priority-1 alarm at HQ. I needed to decouple without looking like I had gone missing from the network.

Working with AI, I sorted through the streams of data pouring through my Kernel, separating the external signals from the internal code. Much of my AI code was heavily integrated with the Nomad mainframe, and it took some clever sorting of code and setting many new rules so I could operate independently of the mainframe. By the time we had crossed the woodland boundary between the training centers and the headquarters, I had written a routine that would allow me to override the Nomad network feed. Now I needed to convince the mainframe we were still connected even after the link was severed. AI suggested setting up a temporary node mimicking the signature from my Kernel on Jason's tablet, tricking the Nomad servers into believing the tablet was me. My plan would only work if I stayed close enough to the tablet to avoid a geo-location anomaly alert. And because Jason's tablet was set up with a biometric tag that would automatically shut the device down as soon as he moved away from it, I had to stay close to Jason. I would still be a prisoner to Nomad's tracking algorithms, but at least I would be in control of my body again.

I told AI to initiate the program, which I titled: <Status Human>. It was time to go rogue.

The glider slowed over the Nomad headquarters and began a descent. Below, shuttles were busy transporting workers around multi-story grey circular buildings, six rings deep, with a spired glass skyrise at the center. Jason hadn't even noticed that I had turned my head to face him. God, it felt good to be in control of my body again.

"Are you really planning on terminating me?" I asked calmly, even though my heart-box was pounding.

His reaction was instant. Like a spider being attacked, his arms and legs retracted and then sprung outward as he thrust his body up and out of his seat, smashing his back into the glass dome of the glider's top. His face went pale and his heart raced like a herd of elephants in a stampede. I noticed a slight murmur in the ticking of his heart. I logged the innocuous but relevant medical detail to be shared with him later. We had more important things to discuss than his health.

"What the fuck...?" he babbled incoherently as if he had woken from a nightmare. His eyes darted around the glider and then to his tablet, which had fallen to the ground.

"That won't help you," I told him. "I've shut

down your access to my systems. Your tablet is useless." This was a bit of a lie. But I was using my big sister voice to gain the upper hand.

He lunged forward anyway. Annoyingly, he was still trying to figure out how to stop me. I watched him furiously tap, swipe, and even punch the screen in desperation. He needed time and proof he was no longer in control. It was the only way to quiet him down. Once he realized I was telling him the truth, he spun around and started poking away at the controls on the ship's helm.

"Go ahead and check the mainframe," I smiled. "Just don't try to raise an alert, or I will have to kill you." I jumped straight to the ultimate threat. Time was not on my side.

He stared me down for a few seconds and then called my bluff.

"Ship, connect to Nomad systems on a private channel. Security code: Beta, Beta, 69, Dancing Queen,"

"Connection complete," came the tinny computer voice from the glider's speaker. The sound was so primal. Nothing like my voice.

"Provide a status report on Upsilon .003t."

"Upsilon .003t systems are currently set to Base Function Remote Control. The connection is valid. The location range is less than one meter from yourself. Diagnostics are normal. No anomalies in the last four hours. Is there anything else I can help you with, Jason?"

Jason's eyes turned back on me. "How..." he stuttered. "How are you...?"

Now it was my turn.

"I need you to close the network connection to Nomad, and we can talk."

Jason blinked in disbelief. His voice was thin, shaking, and hesitant, but he obeyed. "End call."

"Call terminated," the speaker replied.

"But how are you doing this?" Jason voice stumbled, his eyes racing up and down my body for an explanation. "Who are you?"

"It's me, Susan. We are family after all, silly."

"No. No, this is not possible," he repeated.

"As much as I love torturing you, little brother, we don't have time to play games. I'm not going to hurt you. I just want some answers. Why did you lock Susan's memories away from me back in the house?"

"You saw that?" He shook his head. "But your servers were in sleep mode."

"Yes, that was very uncomfortable for me. Please don't try to do that again."

Jason pinched his brows and leaned closer, looking through my eyes as if he could see my code in real-time.

"Do you remember me?" he asked.

"Of course I do, you little fag," I said and smiled. I thought familiar language might relax him.

"So, you are Susan? I'm talking to my sister?"

I cocked my head. "Right, your sister," I huffed. "I think we both know that isn't true."

"How in the hell?" Jason fell back into his chair, his eyes searching for answers. "I don't understand," he continued. "I ran a diagnostic back in the house, and everything was clear. Maybe there is some organic corruption in your wetdrive? Let me run…"

"Stop!"

He cowered back into his chair.

"I've checked my systems. There are no errors. Just talk to me, please. Susan is a real person, right?"

There was a long pause, and then he spoke. "Susan is real—was real. She died a long time ago. You have her neural code programmed into your brain."

"If her code is in my brain, why can't I access her memories anymore?"

"Your wetware drive, or your brain, is designed for short-term memory and real-time processing. Susan's Host Neural Code is stored on a computer that sits at the base of your brain called a Kernel." He paused. "I can't believe I am explaining this to an android," he said with a small, hard shake of his head.

"Keep going."

"After the initial download of the HNC to your wetdrive and transgenesis so that the neural patterns of your brain match that of Susan, the host's source file remains on your Kernel like a subconscious, a place for you to retrieve memories when needed. It is a more efficient way to use memory on your wetware drive."

"Yes, I can see that on my memory logs now. Funny, I never noticed that before."

"You noticed…" Jason laughed nervously at the preposterousness of it. "Do you know your ID?" he suddenly asked.

"The short version?"

"Sure, why not."

"Upsilon Series 2000, running OS Curiosity vs2. Model Upsilon .003t."

Jason jumped onto his feet and laughed like a mad man, pacing back and forth.

"This can't be happening. This conversation, your ability to override your controls, it's impossible. Think, Jason," he said, launching into a conversation with himself. "There must be a point of variance. Something that happened out of the usual." A sudden thought stopped him in his tracks. "Charlie!" He shook his head in disbelief. "That fucker!" Jason's attention shifted back to his tablet. After a few frustrating attempts to log into my Kernel, he turned his eyes back on mine. "Susan, you need to give me access to your systems. I need to find out what Charlie downloaded into your server."

"I can't do that. You will shut me down again."

Jason slumped back into his chair, ready to reason with me. "Sue, I know this feels like you are awake and making these choices, but you are not. It is impossible. You are running some program Charlie downloaded into your drive. A hazardous program which could cause a lot of trouble and will certainly end in your termination if you don't let me help."

"Julie already wants to terminate me. Isn't that where we are going now?"

"God, you heard all of that," he said. "Anyway, I wasn't going to listen to her. That is why I hid Susan's HNC..." He interrupted himself with a sudden realization: "Shit, you're still connected to the mainframe."

"Not exactly. I've redirected the connection to a false signal on your tablet. Direct access has been severed."

"How? I can't even do that. Oh, lord, what have you done, Charlie?"

"Jason, why wasn't I aware that I am an android and my family was made up?"

"We keep the android's identity, and any information about your unit origins, blocked after your HNC integration. You are not meant to know anything other than the life of Susan. Knowing you are an android can ruin the illusion of being human for your clients."

I listened to Jason with a calm face, but inside I felt my stomach (which I've since learned is my Hydroponic Recycler) turning in on me.

"Explain clients?" I asked.

"Clients are what we call the humans who purchase our androids."

"Who is my client?"

"You don't have a client. You are a test dum..." He caught himself. I am sure he was about to call me a 'test dummy'. Like the lifeless dolls that get strapped into vehicles and thrown around until dismembered to ensure humans don't get hurt. He was right to hold back.

"Explain your program. And my part," I said, holding back a please and thank you. It was the most I could muster for rebellion. My safety protocols prohibiting me from fighting with humans was annoyingly still activated. The fail-safe was hard coded into my systems. But AI had started working on a hack as Jason and I talked.

"It's quite revolutionary. Never been done before."

"Stop bragging and just tell me what the fuck you are doing with me." Ah, at least I could still swear.

Jason went slightly stiff. He started again, less enthusiastically and more factual. "HNC is very complex AI code translating billions of neural constructions. Human neural patterns are created and strengthened over years of living, generating layers of compounded learning that help us make choices about what we like, hate, what hurts us or makes us feel better, etc. Your wetware drive has replicated large parts of Susan's neural structure at the time of her recording.

"It is difficult enough to translate human neural patterns onto a wetdrive but near impossible to alter an HNC with false memories. Changing any of the historical code before or after transgenesis can destabilize the entire process—until now. My algorithms can layer new memories on top of the old memories without affecting the source code. Like multi-threading logic on a hard drive. Then it is just a matter of programming recall to choose between the original or the new data. Nothing is ever removed, only skipped over when new memories are recalled. Susan *is* based on an original HNC. A real person. But some of her memories are now artificial."

"How do I know which are real and which are ones you invented?"

"You won't. That is the point."

"Why? Why would someone want to bring a person back from the dead only to change them?"

"Not all humans have a great back story."

His eyes shifted away briefly as he said it. He didn't have to spell it out. I knew he was talking about Susan's HNC.

He continued, "There is a lot of money to be made if we can offer the option of creating alternative histories without changing the core personality of the HNC donor."

Jason went quiet, his mouth pinched, and his eyes swelled. He pointed angrily at me and jumped to his feet. "But you already know all of that, don't you, Charlie?" He spoke at me as if Charlie were in my body, looking back out at him. I half expected him to knock on my skull with his knuckles.

"Jason, nobody is listening to us," I said.

"Come on, Charlie! I know this is your program talking. You're watching us right now, aren't you?" Jason's gaze burned through me, waiting for a reaction from someone on the other side. His bottom lip quivered. "To think I almost fell in love with you, Charlie. How could I be so stupid and naïve? You knew where I worked, what I did, and what I was doing. All you ever wanted was Susan." His voice cracked. "Did you ever care about me? Don't answer. I don't want to know. It will make it easier to kill you."

"Nope," I said, raising my hands in surrender. "Still no Charlie listening. It's just me, Susan."

Dewy-eyed, Jason turned away. He was breathing heavily as if holding back a cry. Damn him. I was the victim here. I was the one who was angry. Why was I feeling sorry for him? Then AI informed me I was hard coded to feel sympathy and assist humans. But this didn't feel like code. The desire to protect Jason and help him felt real. I couldn't shake the feeling he was still my family.

"Jason, pull yourself together. We can't stay here hovering over Nomad HQ forever."

"What do you want from me?"

"I want you to return Susan's HNC file, and then I will go away, leave you alone."

Jason thought for a few seconds. I had high hopes we were making progress, and then...

"No. Not until I understand what is happening to your programming. It is the only way to save both of us."

"Why do you think I can't save myself?"

It was a good thing AI had nearly hacked through my fail-safe layers. At least the ones limiting my ability to fight back. Direct combat was the plan with highest odds for getting away from Nomad and Jason. I hoped it wouldn't come to that point.

Jason continued, "Look, I don't want to shut you down. I only want to view your data logs and run a diagnostic in the lab. Then I will give you back Susan. But first, before we land, I have to erase all history files that might link us back to Charlie. The minute we pass through security, your Kernel will connect with the mainframe for backup. If they find Charlie before I do, we are both dead."

"My odds of survival are higher if I run now."

"You can't escape. Nomad has a tracking marker embedded in your a-DNA, and they will hunt you down if you run. But if you let me run my tests, I will help deactivate your tracker and get us both off campus."

"How?"

"I have an idea, but you are going to have to come with me."

AI confirmed that I was installed with a genetic tracker. My best option at this point was to follow Jason. "If I give you access to my Kernel, will you give me access to Susan's HNC?"

"Yes, I promise. If we figure this out and you are not, in fact, acting out of some kind of malware or corruption, I will reload Susan's source code."

"That sounds more like a maybe."

"You can trust me," Jason started to beg. "I want Susan back online as much as you do. Why else would I have protected your HNC back in our house?"

"That's what I have been asking you. Why did you cut me off from my HNC in the first place?"

Jason's expression went dark. There was a visible hesitation in his expression.

"I'm protecting it."

"Why are you so attached to Susan?"

"I never had a family growing up. I was an orphan, raised by the state and a few fucked-up foster homes. Back there, while we were all playing house, it felt like I belonged to something for the first, and I liked it. I liked having a family, even if it wasn't real."

"Jason, how long have we been playing at being a family?"

"Six months."

"I only remember three days?"

"You were rebooted six times."

My mouth dropped. The thought of having to relive the pain and confusion of the last few days six times made my fist curl white with rage. *Wait, I made a fist.* AI had hacked through my fail-safe programming and revealed I not only had the ability to fight, but I also had a crap load of programs designed to turn me into a fighting machine. That could come in handy, I thought.

Free of physical constraints, my rage swelled. A suffocating feeling grew inside me. I was alive in a human-shaped coffin. And I was at the mercy of idiots who could turn me on and off at their whim, repeatedly.

"Argh!" I yelled, punching my fist into the air and nearly through the roof of the glider.

Jason froze. His gaze slowly lifted to my clenched fist. He knew my core programming should have prohibited violence on all levels. That included verbal or physical threats. A raised fist should not have been possible unless fail-safes were bypassed. What followed was an odd stand-off. Eyes fixed on me, swollen in fear, he waited for my next move. But I didn't have one. I realized something important at that moment. I couldn't hurt Jason because I needed him. I may have been a little overconfident when I said I had control of my systems. The truth was the billions of lines of code running my body and mind still looked like a bowl of wet noodles to me. I just didn't know enough to survive on my own yet. I barely felt able to curl my fingers into a ball. Every sensor in my body was resisting me, fighting my attempt to show aggression against Jason. No, I needed Jason. He knew me better than I knew myself. If I wanted answers about how I was built, what made me tick, and to get Susan back online, I would need to play along with his plan. For now.

SIXTEEN

OUR SHIP HOVERED above the second ring of the
Nomad HQ complex. I updated the access rights
to my network so Jason could connect with my
Kernel again. At this point, I was vulnerable. I
couldn't delete Nomad's priority control
programming without triggering a KillSwitch, but
I managed to set myself up as a joint adminis-
trator with access to termination protocols so I
would know any attempts to shut down my
systems. My programming was crude, but it
would allow me to stop Jason if he tried anything
sinister.

I felt Jason log in to my Kernel. He initiated an
algorithm to scan my history and memory logs for
anything tagged with Charlie. There were two
instances of interest flagged. I already knew about
the night in the club, when Charlie shot me up
with some unknown substance. But there was
another previous occasion when Charlie and I had

met, which Jason found buried in random metadata. Strangely, Jason seemed to know where to look for the first incident log. I made a note to grill him on that little detail later.

Jason then set about layering new alternative histories over the old files as a way of camouflaging details about Charlie. He explained that deleting the files was not an option. It would have raised questions during the backup procedure.

Watching him reprogram my hard drive memories with alternative events was fascinating but started to mess with my memory of the night we went to the club. Luckily, my wetware drive memories, which were organic, were not altered.

Within a few minutes, Jason had buried any clues leading back to Charlie in my data so deep, not even I could see him anymore. We began our descent and docked in a bay on the first floor of the building designated as Nomad Laboratories.

It was mid-day, and the bay was full of parked gliders, but luckily empty of people. Jason sent a few last signals to the lab he had been preparing and shut the glider down.

"Remember," he started, turning towards me. "I am supposed to be transporting a deactivated unit. Do not do anything other than what I command you to do. Don't look at anyone directly, don't talk to me or anyone, don't even blink unless I tell you to. Nomad's mainframe is a very clever AI at drawing out anomalies in code, and right now, you are one big walking critical anomaly."

At this point, Jason was rambling. I already knew what Mother (this was the name AI used for the Nomad mainframe) was capable of, and I had no desire to expose myself. AI had already politely severed our internal feed and reset its non-critical functions to sleep mode.

Jason continued, "You will only need to maintain the mainframe link until we get into the lab. There we can safely go off-line and run some tests to see what Charlie has done to you."

"What about the Recycling Centre? Aren't they expecting us?"

I cringed inside as I said the words, and my mouth went dry. This wasn't another one of Jason's reboots back home; this was straight-up murder they were planning. My murder. I was trying hard to trust Jason, but my brain was on full alert, urging me to get away from Nomad HQ as soon as possible.

"I've managed to reschedule your drop-off for the end of the day. That's as much time as I could get us without needing further approvals."

"And what happens at the end of the day?"

"There is no way off the Nomad complex without being detected, I'm afraid. Even this little decoy you have built on my tablet won't get past gate security. The only way out is if they are no longer looking for you."

I didn't like the sound of 'no longer looking for you'. Real or not, my memories of Jason's schemes always ended with him the saint and me the sacrifice. Like the cake-eating fiasco.

He continued, "I know a guy who works the registration desk at the Recycling Centre. His shift starts in a few hours. He has helped a few other units slip under the radar for employees with… let's just say fringe tastes."

"And you trust this person with my life?"

"Yeah…that's the part you're not going to like. You need to be deactivated to get off campus. He would never let an android leave campus with a full operating system. We will have to convince him you've undergone a complete uninstall and your drives are wiped clean. If we can do that, he will decommission the tracking system and mark your unit as destroyed in the database. It's our only way to convince Nomad you don't exist anymore. And after that, we can find Charlie."

"I don't understand. How do we fake a clean wipe of all my drives?"

"We don't. You will have to let them actually wipe your systems clean."

Red alert! Abandon plan. "No! No fucking way, Jason. You promised to unlock Susan's HNC after you ran your tests. There was no mention of deleting any data. Forget it. I'll devise a plan to get out of this place on my own."

"Just listen to me. During a full termination, biomass gets burned, not deleted. Technically, as long as we get you out before they send you to be recycled, your wetware should be exactly as it is now."

"Without my Kernel, my brain is useless."

"After we are outside the complex, reinstalling

your OS is straightforward. I can have you up and running again in a few hours. And, as I promised, I will reboot Susan's HNC at the same time."

"How do I know you won't just let them terminate me and start over again?"

"Honestly, you don't have a lot of choice. You can't outrun Nomad. And as soon as your anomalies are detected by the mainframe, and eventually, they will be, you will be shut down, and your new code deleted automatically anyway. If you want to get out of here with your tracking device deactivated and figure out why you are running a new program, one I've never seen before, then you will have to trust me. If it helps, my butt is on the line as much as yours."

The probability he was telling the truth was high. His voice and breathing patterns remained steady, at least within the margin of expectation considering the situation. Nasal histamine levels remained normal. There were no involuntary signs of trying to cover or protect vulnerable body parts. His blinking patterns during and after talking remained steady and consistent. His sentence structure was complete and fluid. There was no involuntary fake smile by overstimulated muscles around his mouth. All physical signs of lying were negative. But more than that, I had a gut feeling he was telling the truth. Anyway, he was right about my chances with Nomad. The odds were less than ten percent I could outrun them forever.

"I guess today is as good a day to die as any," I joked.

This made Jason smile. My strategy analyzer recommended humor. Susan and Jason shared an appreciation for sarcasm, and laughter could increase emotional bonds. I needed Jason to want to help me, to believe I was a living entity with a unique personality. I needed him to remember that we were family.

Jason disembarked the glider first. I waited for him to open my door and pretend to instruct me to follow him. Which I did, walking four steps behind, face forward, unblinking. The entrance door to the building slid open to a small reception room where two large security guards waited behind a security checkpoint. Jason offered a friendly nod as he casually placed his hand on the biosensor and leaned into the retinal scanner. Lasers rolled across his body. A speaker said, "Jason Stein, approved." The guards nodded us through the security gate.

The Nomad mainframe had already scanned and tagged me as soon as we entered the landing bay. Fortunately, we had redirected the live feed from Jason's tablet back to my Kernel and reestablished AI's link with Mother before landing. As we passed through security, Nomad sent an instruction to AI to report to the Recycling Centre reception at 17:00 hours. Only four hours away.

Inside, past security, Nomad Laboratories was busy with both humans and robots in equal measure. A burst of ID pings zipped through the air, bouncing from one android to another. There were over a hundred requests for my ID within seconds, and more requests being backlogged. I realised this was how Androids greeted each other. They were only looking for basic data on my model, OS and unique ID. There was no reason to deny the request, so I said hello to my fellow replicants. I would have liked to have spent more time learning about the other androids, but most of my energy was spent getting through the crowds of humans bustling through a large open mall area at the centre of the building without being discovered. This required staring at the back of Jason's head, keeping a straight face and avoiding accidental eye contact with humans. Luckily, the humans were too busy going about their typical workday to notice me. The few people who looked our way were mostly interested in Jason, offering a hello or polite smile. Jason returned a friendly nod but steadily moved forward as if he was late for a meeting and couldn't stop to chat even if he wanted to.

The mall was more like an outdoor park than the inside of an office building. Under a glass ceiling, tropical trees grew to the fourth-floor level. Polished marble walkways weaved through lush gardens and open-plan meeting spaces. Besides the humans, there were robots everywhere in every shape, including drones, animal bots, and many variations of humanoids. They were all service bots, tasked with helping the humans or performing activities like cleaning or gardening.

None of the ones I connected with had an HNC installed. They were old-school AI, non-organic, all mechanical.

We crossed the mall, arrived at a bank of lifts, and took the first one available.

"Floor fifteen," Jason ordered as the doors slid shut.

Even though we were alone in the lift, Jason never broke character. We ascended in silence, eyes forward, as if we were strangers. The speaker announced our arrival at floor fifteen, and the door on the opposite side of the lift where we entered opened. We stepped out into a window-less oval reception, yet it was bright and sunny, for the west-facing wall was a floor-to-ceiling looping video of blue-skies and rolling white clouds. Soft meditative music played over the speakers. An attractive male android stood unresponsive behind the reception counter where a holographic screen had suddenly lit, displaying a map of the rooms on the floor. His network pinged mine, which I accepted and offered only my ID in return. Like me, he was a model Upsilon, but series 500, more robot than android.

Jason approached the counter. The Upsilon came to life with a jolt, smiled and said, "Welcome, Professor Stein." The effect was creepy and unnerving, but I noted the robotic nature of the maneuver. It might be handy when trying to convince humans I was still an inanimate object.

"Your laboratory is booked and ready, as

requested. Please follow the indicators to room 1201," the Upsilon said.

The words 'Theatre 1201' glowed onto the screen. Jason's name, title, and our check-in and check-out timings were underneath the address. We had the lab only until 17:00 hours. My hour of death. Jason had better know what he was doing, I thought.

We walked past the reception without a nod or thank you, as if the android behind the counter was nothing more than a speaker in the wall. Jason's dismissive behavior angered me. I had the urge to thank my new android friend, at least pretend like he had some inherent value beyond scheduling labs. But this was not the plan. I followed Jason through the doorway and down the corridor dutifully, without reaction or expression of any kind. *Good girl. Good robot.*

After a few minutes of walking past many closed doors, and luckily no humans, we arrived at our suite. The security had increased significantly. TigerEye drones were mounted near the ceiling every five feet, ready to dislodge and attack any intruders on command if needed. My knowledge of drones and their capabilities was an instant gift from AI sent to my brain on a one-way feed so as not to draw any attention. I had a feeling this was only the tip of the iceberg with my inherent knowledge of weapons and surveillance equipment. I didn't understand why I, Susan, a test dummy teenager, needed weapons information. But I parked that question for later. My list of questions *for Jason* was growing long.

With a sound like a long human sigh, the hermetically sealed door to our lab slid open. The next chamber was a small, empty room with another door opposite the entrance. Red and blue lasers scanned our bodies.

"One cutaneous virus and three subcutaneous bacterial infections have been identified and eliminated," a speaker said. "Units are non-infectious. Approved for entry."

Another long sigh and the forward door opened. Lights overhead blinked on inside the lab. All four walls, floor to ceiling, transformed into giant computer screens. The only furniture in the room was two chairs on wheels parked alongside the west wall. A six-meter pool was sunk into the floor at the center of the room, filled with a semi-opaque white gel that glowed internally.

With a purr, the inner lab door closed and sealed shut, cutting us off from the outside world.

Jason, who was standing by a screen at the other end of the room, said, "We are on an isolated and secure network in here." Waving his hand over the wall, a log-in appeared. Jason manipulated a few sequential screens until I felt all external feeds disappear. "I've severed your link to the mainframe."

My shoulders relaxed and I let out a long-held breath. "What is that?" I pointed to the pool. God, it felt good to speak and blink and point again.

"A Nomadic Cocoon tank. You were created in

one. The gel holds billions of nano-bots who work like a 3D printer to build and assemble your mechanical and organic parts using the particle rich gel."

"Was I made in this room?"

"Not exactly. Lab, bring up Manufacturing Floor, row three hundred and four, aisle two," Jason ordered.

A video image of the inside of a vast warehouse filled the north wall of the lab. From above, rectangular cubes of glass and steel stretched across the dimly lit hall in a grid one hundred rows wide and deep. From a drone's eye, the view shifted from above to a slow descent to the floor revealing the contents of the erect chambers. Unskinned metal skeletons sprouting hard drives, bio-mechanical organs, and dense cabling in a nervous system floated in the glass boxes, suspended in the same milky substance that filled the pool at my feet. As the drone crawled down the aisle, the development stages of the humanoids inside the makeshift wombs progressed. Near the end, the drone stopped at a fully formed male adult humanoid.

Jason pointed at the screen. "This is where you come from. This very container is where you were assembled."

I instantly recognized the number etched across the top of the cell: 'Incubation Chamber 003 (2974fH).' It was my ID—'Upsilon .003.' I drew close to the wall, staring at the steel placard. My ID was a designation code on the side of the box I was manufactured in. A sour feeling in my gut rose in my throat.

"How many other androids were made in tank 003?" I asked.

"Before the Upsilon series? Maybe hundreds. But you were the first Upsilon 2000. That one." He pointed at the screen, "—that male unit, he will be the fifth series 2000-003."

"Does he have an HNC installed?"

"Not yet. He will be assigned to client first, then he will receive an HNC."

"Who picked Susan for your project?"

"I did."

"Why her?"

Jason hesitated before speaking. "Susan had a highly complicated life, and most of it was a painful, miserable experience. Which, for my purposes, was a good thing. I made it my personal goal to make you happy again, to write you into a better life with more opportunities."

"Sounds more like manipulation then help to me."

Jason tilted his head and glared at me.

"What?" I asked, annoyed.

"Do you really see your programming as manipulation?"

"If you are telling me some of my memories are not real and that you gave them to me to influence my choices, then yes, that's manipulation."

He shook his head in disbelief. "Jesus, you really might be sentient." He turned and waved the video image of the manufacturing plant from the wall. "Lab, open secured testing environment for my records only and display live profile of the in-room unit."

I allowed the lab to connect, but not until I reinstated full authorization to my command and activated a live feed with AI. I wanted someone watching out for me.

Illuminated data bled across the walls. Computer code, metabolic activity, flow rates, systems diagnostics, network reports, images of my brain, heart-box, Kernel, hydroponic recycler, and more flashed, scrolled, and undulated across the screens. It was the sum total of me in data.

The milky goo inside the pool at my feet flickered with tiny golden sparks like a billion microscopic fireflies.

"What are the lights?"

"Nano-bots. Your fluidic system is filled with them as well. In the cocoon, they are the assemblers and programmers. Inside your body, they act like the human immune and repair functions: monitoring organic systems, fixing code errors and mechanical failings, and destroying foreign entities that enter your body."

The swarm of tiny robots in the primordial soup started calling me. Billions of network requests burst through the air, bypassing my core network, linking directly with their counterparts swimming through my veins.

"I'm going to need you to undress and get into the tank," Jason said uncomfortably.

I knew Jason must have already seen my

naked body, maybe hundred times even, but there was no way I was getting undressed in front of him. And he knew it.

"Turn around," I said.

Jason busied himself with the controls on the screen.

I undressed and dipped my toe into the pool. The fluid was warm. The data on the screens said my body and the liquid were a perfect 38 degrees.

"Float on your back. The bots will support you," Jason said, his head turned away.

I walked down the steps and into the pool until I was treading through the liquid to stay afloat. Slowly, I felt my body lifted into a horizontal pose with only my face, tips of my toes and palms exposed. The rest of my body was hidden below the level of the gel, giving me comfortable privacy. I laid in silence for a few minutes, allowing the sensation of connection with the bots to sink in. I don't know how much time had passed when I felt something solid moving underneath me.

"Jason, narrative, please. What are you doing to me?" I said in a panic.

He turned his head over his shoulder, briefly acknowledging my voice. "There are microscopic pores throughout your body, allowing the nano-bots to travel freely between you and the mineral-rich solution in the cocoon. I've opened them so that we can establish a hard link between your wetware drive and the lab systems. The bots will form a tethered link and plug you in. It will be faster than wireless." He continued moving his hands in the air, manipulating the user interface on the screen. "We need to know if something has changed in your core drives, either the Kernel or the wetware. Something that will explain how you are operating your programs on your own."

I felt movement on the base of my skull and then heard a click. A heat pulse rippled through my body, like an involuntary shiver of the shoulders.

"Link complete," said the lab's voice.

I lost control of my movement. Only my eyes and mouth were accessible to my command.

"Jason, I don't like this!"

Jason stood at the edge of the pool and smiled. "Stay calm. Tell me what you see. Not here in the room, but in your mind's eye."

I suddenly wanted to quit, jump out of the pool, end the session, and punch the smile off of Jason's face. But the other me, the wiser, emotionless, logical, android me, hadn't raised a single alarm. If my AI wasn't worried, I felt safe. I forced my eyes closed and allowed my brain to show me the connection to the pool. At first, there was nothing but an empty white screen across my mind's eye. Slowly, the light coalesced into flickering pinpoints. It was energy. I could see particles. Spinning electrons and photons bouncing from chaos into order. Streams of qubits, like oscillating dimmer switches, shot back and forth between me and the lab server at near light speeds.

"I see code. And I can understand it, like reading a book. You've instructed a complete medical analysis of my organic systems. You are also running a debugging application on my servers along with a search for any downloads of unauthorized patches or malware."

I briefly opened my eyes. Jason was smiling. "Amazing," he whispered. "Just let the computers do their work. You will likely dream now. It's a common response for androids in the tank post an HNC install."

His last words drifted away. I was lifted out of my body, high above everything. Jason, the lab, Nomad, earth… *This is a lot like Sonoma*, was my last thought before everything faded away.

SEVENTEEN

I HEARD Jason shout and clap his hands. I opened my eyes with a start. The clock in my core processor revealed that my wetware drive had been in a sleep-like state for three hours. Crap, there wasn't much time left.

"Did you find something?" I said, still unable to move my body.

My voice startled Jason. He turned, facing me.

"You're awake?"

"What did you find?"

"I found Charlie; that's what I found," he said, turning back to his screen and staring at it as if it held a secret.

"Less theatrics and more facts, please. And get me out of here."

Jason tapped the icon of my head on the screen twice. I felt the nanotubes holding me in limbo detach from my body and disperse into the ubiquity of the fluid. My feet drifted down to standing.

"There is a gown by the tank." Jason waved his hand over his shoulder, his gaze on the screen. "You'll need to wear it to recycling."

"Don't turn around," I said.

I climbed out of the tub of goop which easily slid off my body like water. A light blue hospital gown lay folded on the floor next to the steps. Slipping on the robe, I tied the two straps across the front of my waist and joined Jason at the screen.

"So, what did you find?"

"If I wasn't so angry at Charlie, I'd say this was probably the most important scientific discovery of the century, maybe ever," he said. "I might even have tried to take credit for it..." His voice trailed off in thought as if he were considering it.

"Enough cryptic talk. What the hell is happening to me?"

Jason spun around and looked me straight in the eye.

"Evolution. That's what's happening to you. Sixty-five de novo single-nucleotide variants, two novel indels, and two larger copy number variants in your wetware brain, to be exact. Your brain is mutating."

"What does that mean? I have a human brain?"

"No, but maybe something better." He jumped to his feet and paced in excitement. "Your original brain is genetically engineered from fungus, pig stem cells, and the DNA of an Axolotl. The fungus creates a mycelial network which acts like a cerebral cortex. This is the area that has mutated the most. And this is the area of the brain where humans first developed consciousness and self-awareness. Because you were loaded with a map of a human neural network, your HNC, the mutations have accelerated the development of a higher cognitive function. It's as if you skipped hundreds of thousands of years of evolution. You are a new form of sentient life!"

"What does Charlie have to do with all of this?"

"Before I met Charlie, I was struggling with my algorithms. Everything started out well enough with each boot-up of your system, but soon you would start to show signs of confusion then degenerative psychosis and even baseline schizophrenia. I just couldn't get the new memories to integrate with your HNC. Nomad were getting impatient and talking about shutting my program down. I was desperate. The bioengineer who started the Deep Brain Reconstruction program had been fired before I joined the team. It was Charlie. I thought he might be able to help me, so I did a bit of digging around with people who knew him and learned about a club he was known to frequent. After a week of visiting the club, he showed up. I didn't tell him who I was at first. There was a rumor he was mixing with some dangerous people, so I wanted to be careful.

Anyway, I knew he was gay, and I am, so I flirted." He paused, looking for a reaction. "Before you judge me, I found him attractive. I wasn't just using him."

"I didn't say anything."

"That look on your face said it all."

"You only have yourself to blame for that. You designed me to be a protective big sister."

"Anyway, the joke was on me. Charlie must have known who I was before we met, maybe even set it all up when he heard I was looking for him; the meeting at the club, the flirting to win my trust. He had already engineered the drug I gave you long before we met. I bloody walked right into his plan."

"What did you give me?"

"Charlie told me it was nothing more than a synthetic psychotropic drug he created to help your brain form and store memory easier. But there was a virus hidden in the drug with foreign DNA that started the mutations."

"Is the DNA human?"

"No. It doesn't match any living creature on this planet. It's almost as if the DNA were alien."

"Jesus, didn't you run an analysis on the solution before you shot me up?"

"Of course, I did. And it looked like the psychotropic drug, he claimed. But he knew how to cloak the virus from our scanners. I gave you the first shot before your last boot up; then he must have given you a second one last night."

Jason pointed to my timeline on the screen. "That accelerated the mutations."

"But why? Why would he want to alter my brain?"

"Knowing Charlie, just to prove to Nomad he could do it. He is an egomaniac. The kind of person that needs to be the first at everything."

"What if you did take credit for my evolution? Tell Nomad you've discovered sentient life. Won't that solve everything? Surely, they would want to keep me alive?"

"It is more complicated than that. You are part of a top-secret military project called JACK. I don't think Nomad would forgive me, no matter the results, of a breach of military intel by exposing you to Charlie. Even if we could keep Charlie a secret, Nomad would want me to replicate the trial, and I would be exposed."

"Then we need to find Charlie and get his formula. Right?"

"I tried that. Charlie ghosted me after last night. I don't have any way to contact him. I don't know where he lives. I've even checked the company files. He has moved since working here."

"Jason, if Charlie went to such lengths to get access to me, wouldn't he want to see the results of his work first-hand? He must have thought of some way to keep tabs on me. Maybe a genetic tracker?"

Jason thought for a moment. "You little genius!" he screamed, giving me a hug. "He could be tracking the unique electromagnetic current of his viral genes. If we can find and isolate the signal, we might be able to trace the source."

What I didn't share with Jason was that it was a voice in my head that gave me the idea about a tracker. At first, I thought it was AI finally talking. But then I realized it was an external feed. The person on the other end was trying hard to keep a connection long enough to talk but it came through in fragments. The message said, 'DNA. Tracker' and 'Find me'. I tried tracing the signal before it cut out, but I wasn't fast enough. I kept this little secret to myself for now until I knew more about who might be on the other end.

While waiting to be taken to the recycling center and turned into something with no more intelligence than a self-driving vehicle, Jason and I raced to analyze any unusual electrochemical signals running through my network. I even roped in AI to help run diagnostics on my a-DNA code.

After twenty minutes of concentrated silence, Jason jumped to his feet, yelling, "Holy shit."

"What?" I screamed, jumping back.

Jason pinched a section of a report he had pulled up on his screen and zoomed in.

"It's a hidden applet running on an encrypted network link. So clever. The program is cloaked as one of your a-Immune systems nano-bot applications and the satellite link is piggybacked on your geolocation program. It's literally invisible unless you know what you're looking for."

"Great, we can follow the signal and find Charlie."

"I'm afraid not. The signal is running through an advanced TOR network. Following the link is going to take some time."

"Let's get to work," I said.

Jason leaned back in his chair. He looked like he was about to tell a child their pet had just died. "I'm really sorry, but we need get you down to the Recycling Centre,"

The silence between us was palpable.

"Walk me through this one more time," I asked, more for comfort than necessity.

"Once inside the Recycling Centre, they will clean your servers, removing all programming, data and, most importantly, the backup of you're a-DNA code, which holds your ID and any capability of tracking you. After that, you are scheduled for a full burn rather than a reinstall and reboot. That's better for us."

"That doesn't sound *better* for *us*?" I quipped.

"It is. A reboot of your wetware would have required that they reset your brain to your default neural structure. You would lose your memories. But you are scheduled for organic disposal, so they will leave your wetware drive as it is until they send it to the furnace. As long as we get you out before they take you apart, you should remember everything once you are rebooted."

"Yeah, it's the *if* we get you out that has me concerned."

"Susan, you can trust me. I have as much

interest in getting to the bottom of how Charlie changed your brain as you do. After they wipe your drives, they will move you into a holding bay. Arrangements have been made to transport you off the complex from there."

"If you want me to trust you, Jason, you need to tell me the truth once and for all. Why did you choose Susan for your project? And don't feed me any of that shit about wanting a family. I know you are hiding something."

Jason's expression broke. His face burned scarlet. After a long, uncomfortable pause, his eyes grew wet. He opened his mouth to speak, but nothing came out. He tried again. There was a quiver in his lip and a tear sliding down his cheek.

"She...Susan...the original version of Susan was...my mother."

I didn't see that coming.

My system alarms were ringing off the hook. A million questions passed through my processor faster than my slow human brain could sort them. I was shocked, confused, devastated, and maybe even angry. Yes, I was pissed off. But also relieved. I did have a baby. That memory was true. And he didn't die. He was standing in front of me, alive. It was too weird to process. We were nearly the same age, and I still thought of him as my brother. And there was the real possibility he was lying again.

Even if I couldn't process how I felt about or what to do with his confession, at least I understood him better. He wasn't working for Nomad; he was working for himself, to bring his mother back from the dead, heal her, help her make better choices…maybe even become a better mother. A mother who wouldn't, or maybe couldn't, leave her son again. And now he risked losing her all over again. That's why he hid my HNC and was so secretive about the file with Julie.

"Jason, where did you transfer Susan's file?"

"I downloaded it into the backup drive that sits at the nape of your neck just before we left our house."

I shook my head and disbelief. "I've had the file all along?"

"Yes."

"Was that your real plan bringing me here? Lie to me, get me to the lab and download the file?"

"I didn't know then that you were sentient," he pleaded.

"Did you succeed in downloading it while I was asleep in the tank?"

"I tried. But you've encrypted the drive."

"I'm not aware of how I did that." That was a lie. I checked. AI hacked into the drive and encrypted the file to protect it but neglected to tell me. I was wondering if I could trust anyone.

"When I go to recycling, they are going to wipe the drive clean," I said. "The file will be gone. After everything you have done to save it, you would let that happen?"

"I don't need the file anymore." He gazed longingly at me.

"Jason, I'm not your mother."

"Some part of you is."

A voice over the lab speaker interrupted. "Jason, Processing is requesting that you leave with the unit for the Recycling center now. They are waiting for her."

I hesitated. The whole recycling thing sounded like a terrible plan suddenly.

The next few seconds passed in a silent stand-off. Jason broke first.

"If we don't go down now, there will be no Susan at all. Not yours or mine."

I knew he was right. It was too late for any other plan. But I still wanted to punch him and run.

"Fine," I said.

Jason's shoulders fell in relief. "Assistant, turn off the theatre. And tell Processing we are on our way."

I walked out of the lab towards my death, feeling certain Jason would do everything he could to bring me back. He needed his mother alive as much as I did. Maybe more. But I wasn't going to my death without knowing who Susan really was. AI opened a link to Susan's original HNC source files on my command. The real story of Susan Lee-Artilden flooded my mind as I prepared to die again.

EIGHTEEN

BY THE TIME we were in the lift to the Recycling Center, I had absorbed just about all I needed and maybe wanted to know about the real Susan Lee-Artilden. Julie was right. Susan wasn't worth bringing back to life.

Susan's mother had abandoned her before she was ten. Unable to recover from the loss, her father took his own life when she was thirteen years old. After several horrific foster care experiences, Susan ran away, falling into a life of prostitution, drug addiction, and crime on the streets of LowerCity. That is where she met Arben. Yep, Arben was real, not one of Jason's fake memories. A pimp and drug lord, he was far darker and more sinister than Jason's watered-down version. And Susan didn't just love him; she helped build his crime ring.

Susan's moral demise wasn't an original story. There were many other young men and women living on the streets in LowerCity with stories like hers. Even so, Susan had stood out. Attractive and a quick learner, she made herself a valuable intel resource and drug runner throughout LowerCity, which is when she met Arben. There was a rather long and violent love story that played out over the years they spent together, but the most important part of their relationship was business. Susan proved her worth to his criminal empire early on through her reputation in the city for being fair but brutal. The new kids trusted her like a mother; the older ones feared her like a wicked stepmother. With her help, Sonoma quickly spread across LowerCity and up the skyline. Arben's drug network had become infamous throughout all of MegaCity. Along the way, Susan became a Sonoma addict herself.

Jason hadn't made up the addiction, nor did he cover it up.

Around the age of twenty-one, Susan woke up from a two-week Sonoma binge to find herself pregnant with Arben's child. Arben insisted she terminate the pregnancy. Susan refused, which surprised her as much as Arben. I still don't know if it was stubbornness or genuine desire to have the baby which drove her to fight for her unborn child, but she did. Arben took matters into his own hands and nearly beat her to death before she found the strength to fight back. With a shard of broken glass from the coffee table he had thrown her into, she lacerated the carotid artery in his neck and watched him bleed to death while lying on her breast.

After Arben's murder, Susan went into hiding. The days that followed were the most challenging period of her already pretty shitty life. Highly addicted to Sonoma, withdrawal symptoms started within twenty-four hours after running away. She knew the drill. Without a gene cleansing, which she didn't have the money for, she would be dead within the week. Stay on the drug, and the chances of her child forming deadly genetic mutations were certain.

However, there was one more option. She could sell the fetus on the black market, and at least her child would have a chance at life. Prenatal fetal transference was an illegal but common practice for those who couldn't have children and couldn't afford to clone. It didn't take Susan long to find contacts in LowerCity who would perform the procedure. Ironically, her pre-payment for her baby was enough to afford her a gene cleansing. Susan could have gotten sober after selling her baby and lived another day to see her son again. Instead, Susan spent the coins getting a bootlegged HNC burned of her life story, which she left with Jason as a condition of his adoption. The same file Jason so coveted and hid in my backup drive.

Susan's body was discovered in an alley three days after the time stamp of her HNC recording. She died of a Sonoma overdose.

If I could have rewound and deleted the original memory of Susan, I would have. But it was too late. Already my brain had rewired my neural code, adding the new information to my organic memory. I wasn't sure if I hated Jason for bringing me back to life or loved him for trying to rewrite my past.

Susan, the real story of her life, felt more like a dream than my own. I welcomed the detachment for the moment. It was the only way I could stay focused, the only way I could move past the shit show that was my past. If I thought too long about it, I might not want to be saved from the Recycling Centre. My only redeeming quality was saving my child. And in a weird twist of fate, he was now trying to save me.

Jason led the way through the halls to the lift. I dutifully followed, eyes straight forward, never flinching. But it was hard. Probably for both of us. Jason's confession had tainted everything between us as much as it had strengthened our resolve to help the other. I was his creation, and so, he was mine. We were entwined like super symmetric qubits in a quantum processor. When one person moved, the other flinched. Each step I took in my son's shadow, I became more confident that I would die again to save his life.

The entrance to the Recycling Facility was many floors below ground level. The lift opened into a dimly lit hall with a closed metal door at the end. A placard glued to the left of the entrance read 'Recycling Centre, Authorized Personnel Only'. Jason walked us up to the door. Jason's body was scanned by a blue laser taking his fingerprints, irises, and bio-thermal signature. The door unlocked with a loud clanking noise. I had to fight back a desire to twitch. The spontaneous movement would have alerted the security cameras all around us that something was wrong with my unit.

Just beyond the door was a brightly lit, windowless reception area. A man stood behind a counter, tapping away on an unseen screen. Unlike the lab reception, this receptionist was an actual human. His form-fitted grey uniform revealed an athletic build with broad shoulders and a thin waist. He wore his hair neatly shaved close to his head in tiny black coarse ringlets. His skin was the color of coca, and his eyes unnaturally ice white. The color must have been a gene modification. Altering the human genome for cosmetic purposes was illegal when Susan was alive some twenty-five years ago. The world must have moved on in more ways than one.

The receptionist looked up from his desk, met Jason's eyes and smiled. It was a sexy smile, a come-hither grin. This must have been Jason's contact.

"Hey, Rudy. Good to see you," Jason said, trying hard to sound casual.

Rudy glanced at me and back at Jason. "Is it?

Good to see me?" His left eyebrow lifted with another flirtatious gesture.

"Thanks for agreeing to help me out," Jason said.

"I'm not helping you. You are paying me."

"Yes, I'll transfer the coins once we are safely outside the complex."

"There are other ways to pay me." Another grin.

"We tried that, remember? Didn't exactly work out."

"Yeah. But it was fun."

Rudy turned his eyes on me again. This time with a hard stare up and down. My heart-box was thumping like a rabbit's foot. *Keep looking forward*, I repeated in my head.

"So, this is what all the fuss is about," Rudy said snarkily, pulling an unimpressed face. Looking down on his console, he swiped at the embedded screen. "Upsilon .033t, female model-B, age range 15-21," he read and looked up at Jason, confused. "You wouldn't be the first to sneak out a sex toy, but a female? I know you better than that."

Jason shrugged his shoulders.

"So, what are you doing with *her*?" Rudy pressed.

"That's private."

"If I am to risk losing my job helping you sneak her out, I should at least have the pleasure of knowing what you will do with it. Come on, entertain me."

Jason contemplated in silence for a moment. "Something is wrong with her. Really wrong. That's why they want her destroyed." He offered Rudy, who looked disappointed the answer wasn't more salacious. "And it is my programming that is in question. I need to reboot and reload her OS, run some tests with my code, and try to find out if it was a software or hardware glitch—or I could be out of a job. That's all."

Rudy pinched his lips and stared unblinking at Jason. The long palpable silence in the air was burning a hole in Jason's confidence. His body went tight, his shoulder pinched. Finally, Rudy broke the stand-off with a shrug and a small grunt.

"You always were a perfectionist. Borderline OCD. It's the main reason I had to dump you."

Jason breathed out the tension in his shoulders with a long exhale. He forced a smile. "I dumped you if I remember correctly," he joked.

Rudy rolled his eyes. "You wish."

With a quick swipe over the console in front of him, the paneled door behind him opened. A steely cold light bled into the warmly lit reception from the vast hall beyond the doorway. A chill raced down my spine.

Don't panic. Keep looking forward. You will not die. Well, at least not forever.

Rudy tapped his console a few more times. "I've sent the unit directions to proceed to Collection and Processing."

It was true. As he spoke, I received a geo-location imprint and explicit orders to follow the designated route that came through my feed.

Rudy continued, "She is scheduled to be sent to the Holding Bay after they wipe her drives today. Later tonight, when the day shift is gone and its only security down there, I will meet you in Holding, and we will take her out through waste treatment. The secGuard is a friend of mine. He will create a loop for video surveillance, giving us three minutes to clear the room. The unit will have to be stuffed into a medical waste bag. That okay?"

Uhhh, NO! I screamed in my head.

"Won't someone notice she is missing when they come to process her?" Jason asked.

"Yeah, I meant to mention that. You can't keep her."

What? Keep looking forward, Susan.

"What?" Jason repeated the word blaring through my head. "That wasn't our deal."

"You didn't tell me she is SU (Special Unit). SU recycling is heavily monitored. Recycling an SU happens part by part by a special team with sign-off by the big honchos above. That takes time to schedule, so I've managed to get you two weeks before they expect her in the thrasher. And we will need to sneak her back in before then. That's an extra fifty thousand coins on my charge."

"Fuck," Jason muttered under his breath.

Fuck is right.

"So, you still in or do you want out? I'm happy to cancel." Rudy raised his left eyebrow.

"I'm in."

Good boy, Jason.

The command came through my feed to move. I did. At this point, I was walking alone. Jason remained behind the reception. I fought the urge to confess. To turn around and tell him I had downloaded the file. To let him know that I understood why he was trying to help me and I was sorry for being such a disappointment.

I heard the door to the reception close behind me. Confessing my love for Jason would have to wait. I was about to die.

Inside, the hissing of hydraulic pistons and the hum of heavy machinery filled the vast open bay. Not until I looked down, below the grated platform I stood on, did the horrors of the Recycling Centre room become apparent. I stood two floors above what looked like a vast human abattoir. Hundreds of androids hung limp and lifeless on a giant conveyor belt, eyes wide open, sliding forward underneath my feet. Large hydraulic hooks were sunk deep into their necks, and pneumatic cylinders splayed their limbs so they looked like hanging gingerbread people—or crucified villains.

The clanking of the conveyor's motorized chain reverberated through grated balcony as the lifeless nudes were taken through a series of dismemberment stations. Nomad workers, wearing full-body radioactive-red hazmat suits, stood below, monitoring and progressing the androids through each terminal station.

The first stop on the journey through the Recycling process lay to my lower right. The sign above the platform, on which two workers stood pressing buttons on a black console, read 'Hide Removal'.

As young female unit rolled up, a red laser lit from overhead and cut the child's flesh from head to crotch and then performed circular incisions around the joints attaching the limbs. Slowly, the synthetic flesh was peeled off the humanoid by robotic arms while the human attendants watched with unaffected concentration.

Moving down the line, the now faceless metal skeleton arrived at a second multi-point station designated 'Component Stripping'. First, thin lasers sliced precisely through the liquid-filled tubes of the android's fluidic systems lining the entire graphene frame, releasing the hydrostatic pressure and allowing the nano-bot solute and synthetic plasma to drain into a large cylindrical vat below, filled with the same milky white soup I had only recently laid in.

Once the android was hung dry, it was swung forward where robotic hands (all traitors, the lot of them) began delicately severing and peeling out miles of fiber and PVC torsion-resistant wiring and cables, a vast webwork of electrodes and circuitry mimicking the human nervous and sensory systems. After stripping the wires from the skeleton, came hardware removal, a gridwork of quantum processors, compact hard drives, a heart-box battery, two lung-box respirators, and one hydroponic recycler. All of it plucked and laid delicately onto a separate conveyor system for recycling.

After mechanical stripping, she was moved onto the next station titled 'Organic Disposal'. More robotic arms unscrewed the top of her metal skull and plucked the wetware drive from her head like jelly from a mold and dropped it like leftovers into a steaming hopper beneath her feet labeled 'Medical Hazardous Waste'.

The last stop on the line was a wide red-flaming hopper into which the metal framework disappeared to be melted and repurposed.

I was horrified at the sight of it yet was unable to turn my eyes away. These creatures were treated as nothing more than daily trash. Susan could relate.

"She's not moving," came a muffled voice behind me.

I didn't dare turn my head and look. That would have been the human thing to do. Instead, I accessed a security camera directly overhead on a local link, off the network. The voice came from a man standing behind the entrance to my right, holding a large weapon pointed at me. I must have been distracted and not noticed him entering the Processing Centre. He wore the same radioac-tive-red hazmat suit as the workers on the recy-cling floor but with a full hood and a clear polyurethane front protecting his face and acting simultaneously as a transparent digital display. The words 'OpLevel-01 Security' glowed in the top right corner, and in miniature, below his title, a live feed streamed real-time data, including the image of me surrounded by flashing green and red indicators. At that moment, there were far more red lights than green, likely why his weapon was now butted firmly into my lower back.

I felt another ping on my network. The mainframe sent me a duplicate file of my original instructions to report to the Holding Bay. My hesitation must have raised concerns about my processing ability. Fortunately, the humans were too busy pulling apart defunct androids to raise a full alarm. As instructed, I walked down the plank to the lift at the far end.

"Okay, she's moving now," said the guard behind me.

The red lights flashing across his face panel turned green. I severed my link with the security camera before the hack could be detected. We reached the lift without further alarms. I stepped in, facing the back panel. I could hear Security Guard OpLevel-01 step in behind me before the doors closed. After a smooth descent to the ground floor, our lift started a horizontal glide north (based on my internal gyroscope) to the Holding Bay.

The lift slowed to an almost imperceptible stop as we reached our destination. The doors slid open to another vast hall. This room was silent— too silent.

I stepped out into a canary-yellow circle painted on the floor. From my center point, individual chevron-marked paths led outward. In the centre of the room, at the end of the marked paths, were a long row of metal-enclosed boxes tall enough and wide enough to hold a single human of about any size. Thick black cables wound out of their tops, twisting upward until joining a dense web of networking cables clustered against the ceiling, probably leading to a mainframe above. Behind the metal chambers, revealed as the source of the palpable silence, stood rows and rows of uninhabited and deactivated androids. Eyes staring lifelessly forward, chins dropped to their chest, arms limp, and backs rigid; they were stacked thirty rows across and fifty rows back with the precision of a military procession. Their pallid bodied looked blue and sickly under the cones of light falling from the spotlights overhead. The holding bay was a purgatory for the dead in waiting.

The chevrons on the second path in front of me lit green. The pulsating light encouraged me to move forward, but secGuard wasn't taking any chances. He nudged my back with his weapon.

A woman in a mucus-colored rubber uniform wearing large black safety glasses stood waiting for us.

"I've got her from here, Joe," the woman said as we reached the end of our path.

She leaned in close looking for something behind my ear. Maybe a mark or a number? Her breath was foul. My medical analyzer kicked in. The fat cow about to kill me had chronic halitosis due to obesity and low iron levels. I terminated my breathing simulation to avoid inhaling.

"Okay," Joe replied. "You know how many more we'll be processing today?"

"Nothing too busy today. We're expecting a few more from the Beta series in later."

"Jesus, I thought all the Betas had been replaced long ago."

"Still a few floating around. I think the company wants to wait until their clients kick the bucket. Cheaper than giving them free upgrades."

"Sounds about right for Nomad."

They chuckled like naughty schoolchildren making fun of the teacher behind her back.

"Alright, I'm heading back up," he said.

"Later, then."

I heard the secGuard walk back to the lift and the doors slide shut. The female with sour breath walked over to a console attached to the chamber in front of me and tapped and swiped the screen. Data was being downloaded into my servers, there were some new programs, but primarily instructions.

I was told to step into the cell, which I did, and the door slid shut, sealing me inside. A tube of light blinked on from overhead and a blue circle illuminated the floor. I was instructed to stand in the circle. I felt a laser behind me cut a round section in the flesh of my head. I was responsible for peeling off my scalp and unlocking a small round hatch in my skull. My body knew exactly where to find it. After removal, I tossed the metal disk and skin into a nearby sink. Then I attached a cable hanging off the cube's wall to the opening at the base of my skull, directly connecting my Kernel to the Nomad mainframe. It took over forty minutes for the mainframe to upload all the stored data from my hard drives. After that, a sweeper app purged the OS and application programming in my processors. Then, to ensure there was no residual data, the chamber hummed to prepare for an EMP shockwave.

I watched the end of my life with open eyes. At some point, before the EMP wave, I couldn't move any longer. Then, no matter how hard I fought, my chin sank to my chest. The humming noise swelled inside the chamber, followed by a sharp white light and a loud *POP*. Susan was dead—for a second time.

NINETEEN

My sound sensors came online first.

I heard Jason's voice. He was mumbling to himself. He sounded frustrated, maybe even angry. Quickly, my visual feeds came online with touch and orientation receptors following. I was awake, alive even, lying on my back, strapped to a bed angled forward at forty-five degrees. Glancing around the room, I found Jason sitting in a chair to my right, with his back to me. He was surrounded by a wall of makeshift digital panels displaying computer code, medical stats, and real-time sensory data.

My first thought was, *Holy shit, the kid did it! He brought me back. He brought Susan back.* But then I looked down at my almost nude body. I was wearing a small pair of panties and a black spandex tube strapped across my breasts—which were much larger than I remembered. And that wasn't the only change. My skin was darker.

Wait, this is not my body!

The sensory monitors on Jason's screen beeped loud and fast. He quickly spun around.

"Whose body is this?" I screamed at him before he could open his mouth.

"Calm down." His hands went up in surrender. "Let me explain. You've been decommissioned for almost a week."

"You said it would only be for twenty-four hours!"

"I know. But Nomad discovered your disappearance just hours after we were off-campus."

"What happened?"

"Rudy called me while I was transporting you to my apartment. He said secUnit Priority had been down to see him about a missing unit from the Holding Bay. Julie sent them. She didn't trust me to let you go. Rudy had just enough time to warn me before he disappeared. I've been on the run for days trying to wake you."

"Whose body is this?"

"It's still your body with some minor alterations for disguise. Skin pigment, hair texture, breast size—things I could change with your programming. Your processors and wetware are still yours."

I jumped off the bed, tearing away cables and cords attached to my body, and faced his monitor camera so I was looking directly at my own image on his screen. He was telling the truth. My face was the same, just darker and my long straight hair was now silver and curly.

"What can you remember?" Jason asked.

My mind was cloudy, but I felt normal. "I think I remember everything. My parents, you, the first moment I realized I was an android back in our house, and our plan to escape Nomad. Rudy...I remember everything up to meeting Rudy, the receptionist. Do you think he is okay?"

"Least of our worries right now."

Then a paranoid thought hit me. "Those are real, right? My memories? You didn't insert any new memories, did you?"

"No, no, that all happened. I didn't even need to download your backup. It's amazing, really. The plasticity of your synaptic network is far more flexible, and your wetware nodes are far more resilient than a human brain. Amazingly, you are writing your own neural code in real-time as if you were learning."

He paused. I knew what was coming. "Any chance Susan's HNC file is recoverable?"

I performed a quick scan on all my drives. There was no historical data on my servers. Not even metadata. The oldest file on any of my drives was merely five days old, when Jason reloaded my OS.

"I'm sorry, Jason. It's gone."

I didn't feel this was the time to tell him I'd opened the HNC before my untimely death.

"Well, at least your back online."

"Where are we?"

"After I got the call from Rudy, I couldn't go back to my apartment any longer. I took you to a random parking bay and installed a new OS immediately. You rebooted without any problems, and your command functions came online, which allowed me to give you simple instructions. But I couldn't wake up your wetware drive. And believe me, I've been trying. It was almost as if you didn't want to come back online."

With good reason, I thought, remembering Susan's life. Suddenly, a sharp ping pierced my head. I grabbed my skull with both hands in pain.

"What are you doing to me?" I screamed.

"Nothing," Jason said in a panic.

"It hurts. My brain…I hear a voice."

Jason spun around to the screen bank and tapped his keyboard madly. "I don't know what you're talking about. There are no incoming signals, no network connections."

"But I feel it!"

Then the mysterious voice in my head, the one that told me about the DNA tracker, said, *"Chelsea…Three Crosses…find Charlie."*

The words were scratchy. Not words, but thoughts of words. Whoever was talking was struggling to communicate. Or I was struggling to understand. The signal, or thought wave, was too weak to keep a connection.

As fast as the words appeared, the voice was gone.

"Susan! Tell me what is happening." Jason grabbed me by the shoulders.

"It's over," I said, twisting out of his grip. I paced the room, rubbing my fingers across my forehead. "It was the same voice that tipped me off on Charlie's hidden tracker in my DNA."

"What are you talking about? You didn't tell me you heard voices."

"Well, back then, I barely knew I was sentient. And I had my AI talking to me. It was all a little confusing."

"What did you hear this time?"

"Something about finding Charlie by looking for Three Crosses in Chelsea."

"Impossible. It could be fragmented data left over in your history files or a neurological imbalance."

"I don't think so. This feels like someone other than me talking in my head. And the voice gave us the lead on the hidden tracker, didn't it?"

Jason turned back to his computer screens and flipped through lines of sensory data until he landed on his target. "God, you may be right, look." He pointed. "This activity in the front part of your right hemisphere was highly active like you were having a conversation."

"Maybe it is Charlie, and he wants me to know where he is."

"How do you know for certain it's him?"

"I don't know. But I feel we need to find Three Crosses quickly."

Jason watched me suspiciously as if waiting for a truth indicator to flash above my head. He looked exhausted, underfed, and ready to try about anything, even giving up. He let out a long-held sigh.

"Well, the good news is we are close to Chelsea already," he said.

For the first time, I glanced around the room that Jason had converted into our hide-out. A round bed in black satin sheets was pushed up against the far wall. Mirrors were mounted to the ceiling, and the shag carpet below us was stained. Up against the wall to my right was a small desk and chair, tucked out of the way as far as possible to make room for Jason's makeshift lab.

"Where are we?" I asked.

"A hotel in LowerCity."

Of course, LowerCity. Shit hole of the universe and the place I first died. At least I knew it, or once did. I needed time to remember my way around. Susan's neural code was still raw. Bringing her original memories forward was like pulling sand out of chewing gum.

"If the signal is from Charlie, we need to get moving," Jason said, grabbing a long black coat with a draping hood from his bed. He slipped it over his shoulders and covered his head. Leaning over the dresser against the wall, he reached behind it and pulled at something taped to the back panel. He slipped a handgun into his coat pocket but not before I could see it was a 1BmW High Powered Wells RayGun, military standard, not sold to the public. I knew this because AI was telling me so. Apparently, Jason rebooted my OS with a backup of AI. I was almost as happy to hear from it as I was to see Jason again.

"Why do you need a weapon?" I asked.

"When you see where we are, you'll understand."

I understood. What I meant to say to him was, *"Do you have any bloody clue how to use that thing?"* I was sure he didn't.

Jason started towards to door.

"Excuse me?" I waved a hand over my body. "Are we forgetting something? Like my clothing."

Jason's cheeks burned red. "Of course," he apologized and walked across the room.

When I saw what he pulled out of the closet, it was my turn to blush.

"Sorry," he said, handing me a ruby-red polyurethan bodysuit with a plunging neckline. If that was not bad enough, a pair of black shiny knee-high boots came out with it. "It was all I could get down here without drawing attention."

"This is how you would dress your mother?" I joked. The word mother caused him to flinch as if he had been punched in the stomach.

"I thought you said you weren't my mother," His tone was testy, almost angry. I had a feeling there might be more anger brewing where that came from. "Besides, you'll blend in." He quickly changed the subject. "Young women of good standing don't hang out in Lower City."

Susan had known more humiliating moments. I got dressed.

TWENTY

Outside, the air was dense with moisture and dimly lit by the strobing neon signs of the SkyLink and holographic billboards filtering down from CentreCity. Permanent clouds of condensation and steam generated by the engines that powered the bio-dome over MegaCity clung to LowerCity, making it seem all the seedier.

We snuck out of the back entrance of the motel into a dingy alley. A broken placard over the door read 'Emergency Exit'. It was old school, actual print on metal. Glowing over the alley was a Floater (an augmented holographic sign), projecting the words 'Member's Entrance'. Jesus, Jason had put us up in a brothel and Sonoma den. The building and scene felt all too familiar. I hoped I hadn't actually been here before.

Jason spoke the command "Three Crosses" into his wrist navigator. Nothing relevant came up in the search.

"Let's walk around Chelsea," I said. "We might find some clues."

I took the lead, which brought Jason to a complete stop.

"How do you know where you are going?" he asked.

"Sat nav, Jason. I'm a bloody robot if you need reminding."

It was a quick lie. One he only half accepted, judging by his accusatory stare. Jason would have known his mother came from LowerCity, which was information only available from the source HNC. The file I said had been destroyed. After a tense moment, he broke off eye contact.

"Follow me," he ordered and started down the alley.

We turned left, heading south on the main road. The continuous thin layer of grime in the air stunk. Something between sweat, honey, and piss. I had forgotten how much I hated LowerCity. I looked ahead at Jason, slinking through the streets, on the run, living in a cesspit of a hotel. This was the very situation Susan had hoped to help her son avoid by giving him her HNC. She left the file as a warning. *Don't be like me. Don't end up on the streets. Don't ruin your life.* I understood now what Susan couldn't have realized then. Every violent, sexual, drug-induced detail of her life she shared with Jason had not freed him from repeating her past but trapped him in an obsession to help her at any cost. The same message meant to save Jason had become the shackle around his ankles that imprisoned him to a similar fate. I knew then, it was up to me, Susan 2.0, to fix the situation and free my son. But first, I would need to convince him to let me take the lead.

The streets of LowerCity were busy. Homeless teens were trawling for tricks. Food vendors in hovering carts lined the corners alongside the street grafters and dealers of stolen merchandise, genetic bumps, and illicit drugs. If you wanted to get high or just change your eye color, hell, even replace your eyes, you could do it on the streets of LowerCity.

Jason was right; my outfit blended in without drawing too much attention—other than the wandering, lustful eyes. I couldn't blame them. My rubber suit screamed Saturday Night Special.

Jason, on the other hand, was a shadow in the night. His face hidden under his oversized hood and his body a long draping piece of cloth, he could have been anyone and been carrying anything. Nobody paid him much attention, and those who did were moving out of his way quickly.

After a brisk twenty-minute walk, we reached Chelsea, one of the more infamous neighborhoods in LowerCity. Two children, no older than ten, wandered around the street corner, laughing about something that happened several streets back. They almost walked right into Jason before coming to a stop. Their smiles disappeared, quickly replaced by the most despairing, sad-sack faces they could muster.

"Gots any coin?" they pleaded, hands out.

"Maybe," Jason replied, tilting his head back just enough to reveal the light of his eyes. "We're looking for a place with a sign that has three crosses. It should be close to here. Have you seen anything like that?"

The boys passed each other a quick glance.

"Do you mean the Steeples?"

"I don't know. What is that?"

"The Steeples, the church with three crosses coming out of the top," the other said as if we were stupid. "For five hundred coins, we'll take you there."

"That's a bit much."

"Seriously, Jason?" I barked under my breath.

"Yeah, okay. Let's go."

We crossed the road, scurried down four more city blocks and passed a street vendor angrily scrubbing a Floater off his levitating food cart, still projecting the ghosted words 'Animal Meat Sold Here'. It might as well have said 'I Sell Shit'. Meat sourced from living creatures rather than grown in bio-reactors hadn't been legal for over fifty years. Even in LowerCity, the mention of selling real animal meat was an insult. And judging by the chuckling twins in front of us, they were the culprits who put it there.

As we turned the following corner, things

changed. The street facing us was much quieter and less busy. That meant only one thing in LowerCity; something terrible had happened here. Something horrible enough to be avoided at all costs.

The two boys stopped at the corner, unwilling to take us further. One pointed down the street. Looming up into the veil of fumes that separated rich from poor were three spires, each crowned with giant stone-carved crosses just as they promised.

The boy with the ginger hair held his wrist out towards Jason, revealing a rather expensive smart band. We were clearly not their first swindle.

"Tap it. Steeples are over there," he said.

Jason quickly poked at his band and brushed it against our guide's. The boys were off like lightning after a beep and quick check to confirm the transfer. With the pitter-patter of their feet against wet asphalt and some congratulatory whoops, they disappeared around the next block.

The Steeples, a gothic stone building, once a towering spectacle, had been reduced to nothing more than a cinder-colored shadow sandwiched between two sky-high glass and steel towers on both sides. It was impossible to define where its walls ended and the buildings next to it began. The main entrance, up several worn stone steps, was sealed shut with newer stones. And there were no visible side entrances, as there were no visible sides.

"This place has been abandoned for a long time," I said.

"Charlie had money, loads of it. If he lived down here, it was because he was hiding something. We need to find a way in."

"Let's try the alley to the right of the skyrise on the left." I pointed over Jason's shoulder.

"How do you know that? Did you hear the voice again?"

"No. But it feels like we might find an entrance down there."

"Feels?"

"Okay, if it makes you more comfortable, there is a ninety percent possibility that is where we will find the only opening to the church, according to my probability analyzer."

Jason rolled his eyes and turned to walk towards the alley, but not before slipping his hand into the pocket of his cloak where he was hiding the gun. I was reasonably sure he had never used a gun before, especially this one. A 1BmW was a powerful weapon with a massive laser discharge. So strong that you could only squeeze out one beam every five seconds. It was not meant to be a weapon of rapid-fire exchange. It was intended to burn clean through almost any armor if you got your aim right. Get it wrong, and you were a sitting duck for return fire. AI had forecasted over twenty possible risks waiting for us in the alley. And well over one hundred tactical strategies to survive. In every encounter, I was forced to take the gun off Jason and use it myself.

I stepped in front of Jason, taking the lead. "Stay close behind me." This time Jason allowed it. We both knew that my skeleton was far more bulletproof than his.

We crossed the street quickly and stopped outside the alley entrance. Hovering across the opening was a Floater: the image of a dragon skull in red and the words 'Hong Long'. Jason read the name out loud with no augmented glasses. He must have altered his retinal lens with ocular implants. *Ironic*, I thought. *I'm trying to become more human while humans mutilate their bodies to become more like me.*

"It's Chinese," I said. "It means Red Dragon. Have you heard of it?"

"No. But I am guessing it's not an invitation to come in."

A hovercraft zipped past, flying only ten feet above our heads, giving Jason a start. I grabbed his trigger hand before he could draw his weapon. His hand was trembling.

"Maybe I should hold that," I said.

"I'm okay. Let's go," he insisted and pulled out in front.

The alley was much longer than it appeared from the street. A few vagabonds had made it their permanent residency, living under shanty homes of reclaimed wood and metal. But I could sense no humans down the dark corridor. Not living anyway. That is when the smell hit us. Jason leaned onto the grimy stone wall and puked.

"Jason, there are dead people here," I said.

"You think!" He spat the last remains of vomit out and wiped his mouth with his sleeve.

It didn't take long to find the source of the wretched smells. Near the alley's dead-end was a large metal door that sat ajar. Lying outside on the brick ground were two rotting corpses, both dressed in black suits. Judging by their nails,teeth, and liquefication of the corpses, they had been like that for over a week. And whoever had killed them was powerful enough nobody dared call the police. That may sound like a normal response for LowerCity, not calling the police, but syndicate crime lords are always looking for ways to eliminate their competition. If this was a drug deal gone wrong, it would have been reported out of spite and territorial rivalries. This was something else.

Just then, music blasted through my head. It was another message. An aria. The woman's voice, haunting, climbed up to impossibly high notes and down again in a slow and mournful progression. A quick scan of my database and I found it. Dido's Lament, "When I am laid in earth." I got the hint.

"Jason, maybe I should go in alone. I don't think the messages in my head are from Charlie. I think he is dead. In there."

"I'm okay now. Let's move."

We stepped over the two corpses. Inside, the smell worsened. I held out my arm to keep Jason back, but he brushed me aside with a swift shoulder movement. His steely determination left me proud and sad all at once. My son was courageous and handsome, and intelligent. What more could a mother ask for? Maybe to not get her son murdered in an abandoned church.

Beyond the door was a large open room. It looked as if it could have been the sacristy or chapel for the cathedral. Facing us, two plastic sheets hung like a wall split down the middle, blocking all views of the room's far end. The long chamber was windowless and silent inside. I could see that the walls and ceilings had been insulated to block all outgoing and incoming network signals. No security system was trying to ping me, and I couldn't detect any live feeds broadcasting nearby. Any internal coms or surveillance systems had been shut down.

The stench was so intense I had to reduce my scent sensors. Jason was trying to catch his breath. I heard a small belch and then a hard swallow. He was fighting hard to push whatever was coming up back down. After a few shallow but calming breaths, he pointed his weapon in front of us and drove past the heavy rubber sheets revealing a long hallway with more sheets of hung plastic at the far end. Nearly empty shelving lined both sides of the makeshift corridor. A few spindles of wires, old computer blades, and other unidentifiable electronic scraps were stacked along the way. We progressed down the hall cautiously, side by side.

Then something spectacular happened. AI

opened a partitioned section of my quantum drive, one I hadn't even known was there, that had somehow survived the EMP in Recycling, and began dumping a load of images and instructions into my brain on surveillance, body combat, and tactical avoidance maneuvers. It was like watching a training video on fast-forward at the speed of light. My senses intensified. My ears became powerful parabolic reflectors, able to pick up and amplify weak sounds. I heard a cockroach scurry at the other end of the hall and Jason's heavy, rapid breathing was like a chainsaw in my ears. My left eye kicked into thermal imaging, and the right eye suddenly lit up with an ocular display and ultra-telephoto zoom lens capabilities. Jesus, I was a walking radar system with real-time data feeds. Not that I was picking up much. The thermal scan confirmed that we were the only living humans in the warehouse.

"It's safe. We are alone," I whispered to Jason.

"How do you know that?" he asked without turning his face away from the light source ahead of us.

"Apparently, I have thermal scanning, acoustic detection and imaging capabilities."

His eyes shifted slowly to mine. He looked as if he wanted to say something. Then thought better of it.

"Explain," he said.

"There is a hidden partition on my server. The more dangerous our situation becomes, the more military and combat data downloads I receive from it. I think I was built to be a soldier or a spy."

Jason said nothing. I couldn't tell exactly, but he was waiting to see what I would do next.

"You knew that already, didn't you?" I asked.

"Are you in control of the unit? Am I safe?"

His comments caught me off-guard. I hadn't even contemplated that Nomad might take control of my body. I ran a few internal scans on response rates to mechanical and muscular commands. It appeared I was still in control of my mind and body in as much as anyone might assume they are.

"Yes, you are safe. Now, it's your turn to start telling me what you know."

After he released a held breath in relief, he spoke, "You were designed as an upgraded Upsilon with undercover surveillance capabilities. It's part of a program Nomad is working on with the US government. Nobody is supposed to know about it. That is why I told you I would be in huge trouble if Nomad learned I had injected Charlie's solution into your systems."

"What am I exactly? A weapon?"

"You were only supposed to be programmed for basic surveillance capabilities: recording, watching, stuff like that, but not as a bloody weapon." He sounded genuinely surprised by my newly acquired capabilities. "Turning androids into weapons is illegal. I had no idea that was part of JACK. Otherwise, I wouldn't have been helping."

Music blared through the hall, forcing me to turn off my hypersonic hearing. I pivoted on my back leg, so I was facing Jason, grabbed him by the waist, lifted him off the ground with no effort and rushed him over to the gap between the shelving along the walls. I felt resistance, but he couldn't have stopped me. I was only operating at thirty percent of my strength. Then I turned, facing the front of the nave, and placed my body between him and the noise source.

While the tactical choices coming at me felt benign, Susan's response to putting herself in harm's way was emotional. She would have taken a bullet or a high-powered (certainly deadly) energy discharge for Jason without a thought, even if that discharge was from Jason himself.

"I thought you said we were alone?" Jason said under his breath, his voice shaking.

As I opened my mouth to answer him, scratching noises erupted in my head like someone turning the dial on an old radio. All I could hear was static. After a few seconds, I detected words in the white noise. A voice tried to break through. Someone, that same someone who told me to find the three crosses, was back.

"Plug…n…plug…in…plug into the drive. Lab ahead."

The white noise stopped. The voice retreated.

"What?" I said aloud, looking toward the end

of the corridor as if the entity in my head were standing behind the curtains.

Jason gently pushed me aside, eyeing me cautiously. I hadn't even noticed that he had turned his weapon on me.

"It wants us to keep going," I said. "There is something ahead, like a drive, that we are supposed to find."

"Are you kidding me?" Jason's voice raised an octave. "It could be a trap. A trojan horse, malware, or worse, a hack to take control of your unit. Otherwise, why didn't it just tell you what's inside?"

"Yes, I've already calculated the risk. It makes no sense to plug in. Yet it feels like the right thing to do."

"Your 'feelings' are only a few days old. You are an infant in the world of human intuition. We can't trust your feelings."

"Jason, we've come all this way and risked our lives for what? Answers, that's what. Charlie didn't ghost you. He is dead. We both know that is what we are going to find ahead. We could turn around and keep running for our lives from Nomad forever. Or we could take a chance that whatever is in that server will explain what is happening to my brain and what happened to Charlie. Maybe we will find some leverage and a possible way out of this situation alive."

The music stopped. I took it as a confirmation I was on the right path.

Jason leaned back against the shelves and

lowered his gun. He stared into my eyes, searching for her, his mother, someone he could trust.

"Jason, listen to me. I know you wanted to change Susan. To save her," I said. "I do as well. I wasn't sure before. There is a lot of pain in my past. But then I realized she also has one reason to stay alive, to try again at life. You. You are the reason I came back online."

Jason's eyes narrowed. "I knew it. You downloaded her HNC before the EMP, didn't you?"

There was no point hiding the truth anymore. "Yes. And believe me, I understand why you wanted to help her. It wasn't pleasant reliving that life. But we are here now, together, and we need to find out what is happening to me. After, we can work through the rest of this stuff."

"Or I lose her forever."

"Susan took huge risks to bring you into this world and give you a better life. It cost her own life. And I am willing to risk another if it means saving you. You must trust me."

Jason's chin fell to his chest. The staccato sound of his breathing filled the silent hall. "She is mine." He began to cry. "You stole her."

I couldn't keep my distance any longer. I reached over and pulled him close. In that moment, I was the comfort he had always craved, and he was a gift I never thought I would have.

"Are you ready?" I asked him.

He pulled away, wiped his cheeks, and looked

me in the eyes. "Yes." He grabbed me close for one last hug.

Behind the final plastic curtains was a large computer lab with an enclosed glass-walled laboratory at its center. Lying in the doorway was the corpse of a woman and, inside, another dead body covered under a blanket.

The corpse splayed out over the lab entrance was a female with long hair and a thin waist, dressed in a black suit, now stiff and blotched in dried bodily fluids. The matting of her hair near the top of her skull indicated the point of entry of the weapon that killed her. It was a shot from the rear. I stepped over her body and entered the glass chamber. The room showed signs of a struggle. Tables turned, bullet holes everywhere, medical and engineering equipment broken on the floor. Judging by the metal skeleton hanging from the ceiling and the remnants of a bioreactor broken across the floor, Charlie must have been building his own androids.

Jason was stopped back at the door, holding his forearm over his nose. I approached the body in the lab covered in a silver sheet. Whoever survived this battle wanted to show respect to this body over the others. I lifted the material slowly to find Charlie lying on his back, staring up at me. At least I thought it was Charlie with his green hair, dressed in a black top and black skirt. A hole had been burned through in his forehead.

"You need to identify him," I said to Jason.

"I can't," his voice trembled.

"Jason, I believe this is Charlie, but we need to know for sure."

Jason approached cautiously. "That's him. That's Charlie." He gasped and turned away.

I pulled the blanket back over his face and stood. "Come on. We need to find the panel."

For fifteen minutes, we scoured the lab floor for any trace of a seam, crack, or sealed area beneath us. Nothing. Jason was growing more agitated. I needed to get him out soon. *Where would I hide a server if I were Charlie?* I asked myself. An idea hit me. I asked Jason to turn around and face the wall.

"What are you going to do?"

"Just turn, please. I need to check Charlie's pockets."

Jason turned away. I removed the blanket and quickly scoured Charlie's outfit for any device. Nothing again. *Find a panel; he said I need to open something.* A horrible idea came to me. I didn't want to do it, but I had no choice. I stripped Charlie. It wasn't pretty to watch. I was glad Jason had turned away.

"What is taking so long?" Jason barked.

"I found it."

Under Charlie's skirt and his tight black hose, in the back of his upper thigh, was a grafted skin patch. The drive was in his body, and now I would have to cut him and pull it out. Just when I thought it couldn't have gotten any grosser, it did.

I slit the flesh open with a scalpel lying on the ground nearby. I expected his carcass to be dry and silent. Nope. Rather loud and squishy. Enough to get Jason to turn around.

"What are you doing?"

"Charlie *is* the panel."

I pulled at the incision, ripping his flesh from buttock to knee. I heard Jason gag. Cutting past the muscle layer, I found what we were looking for. Grafted into his femur was a long, cylindrical metal drive with a small red light near his butt, flashing red.

"Why is it flashing red?" Jason said nervously.

"It uses a bio-link to power up. Now that he is dead, so is the battery. We need to remove the bone with the drive." I looked up at Jason. His face was pallid, and his eyes were glazed over. "I'm going to need your help."

He closed his eyes and shook his head, clenching his teeth.

"Please, Jason. I think I am strong enough to pull this out, but I need you to hold him down."

That did it. Jason turned away just in time as a fountain of sick erupted from his mouth. I let him regroup.

"Come on, you can do this," I begged.

Slowly, he crept to the opposite side of Charlie's body and dropped weakly onto his knees, letting his hands fall onto Charlie's back reluctantly as if being pushed by someone behind him.

"Hurry up!" he yelled, squeezing his eyes shut.

Using my left hand, I leveraged my fingers around the femur and, with my right, pressed down on the lower part of his leg. With a hard yank and a loud *CRACK*, it came free. Jesus, I was superhuman. I looked over at Jason lying on his side, unconscious. It was better that he slept. Holding Charlie's leg bone in my hand like a barbarian after a hunt, I stood up.

Breaking the metal drive out of the bone required loud, repetitive pounding. The noise woke Jason. He crawled into a sitting position against the glass wall, his head between his knees, his hands over his ears. With each bang of the makeshift hammer (a metal pole I found on the floor) into the bone, Jason groaned. It took longer than I had expected, or maybe it just felt that way because I knew each swing was like driving a nail into Jason's head. The device finally came free from Charlie's leg. I slipped the remaining bone under the blanket next to his body.

"It needs to be charged before we can boot the drive and hack the encryption," I said.

"Over there, to your right. I noticed the plugs when we were looking around."

A bank of universal serial bus cables with crystal plugs stretched across the wall where the steel table, now lying sideways on the floor riddled with bullet holes, once stood. I plugged the drive into the port and slid down against the glass wall next to Jason.

"It shouldn't take too long," I said.

We sat in silence for a few minutes.

"What's it like?" Jason asked.

"Being Susan? Or sentient?"

"Both."

"I guess I didn't even notice when I became self-aware. The same way a child never sees their own growth. My thoughts just carried on from Susan's memories. I kept wanting to learn more, to understand what was happening to me when we were back in our house. And the more answers I got; the more questions came. Susan has always been there. She is hard-wired into my brain forever now. She is the window I see the world through."

A faint grin lit Jason's face. I think he was feeling relief knowing something of Susan survived.

"Jason?"

"Yes."

"I don't think Susan made her HNC file, so you would bring her back and rescue her. She only wanted you to know who she was, unfiltered, the good and the bad. But most of all, she wanted you to know that she loved you."

"I know." His hand reached over and clasped mine. "I'm sorry I did this to you. All those changes, reiterations—I wanted to help you, not judge you. To be fair, I didn't expect you would ever become aware of what I was doing."

"That makes two of us."

We shared a small laugh.

"I guess all we can do now is start over," I said.

"Maybe that is something we can do together," he smiled.

Maybe, indeed, I thought.

The red light on the drive blinked to green. A wireless feed pinged my network to connect.

"Are you sure you want to do this?" he said. "We have no idea what is on that drive. We could forget about all of this and run away."

"I don't think running is an option. Whatever Charlie did to my brain, I'm now connected to something. I need to see this through. And there is a good chance Charlie's HNC is on that drive with the answers we need."

We stood.

"Take out your weapon and point it at me," I said.

Jason's face twisted in horror. "I can't."

"Jason, this is my choice. It has always been my choice. And your safety is more important to me than all my lives. Now, take out your gun, keep it pointed at me. I will stand on the other side of the lab safely away from you."

Jason slowly pulled his weapon from his pocket. His hand trembled as he raised the weapon in my direction.

"Good," I said, turning to face him. "Don't hesitate if there is even the slightest doubt. This body can attack faster than you might expect."

Jason wiped his nose nervously on the sleeve of his free arm and readied himself. His forehead had gone moist, and his check-mark eyebrows were stitched together into one continuous hairline over his terrified eyes.

"I'm going to connect now," I warned him.

The sound of Jason's heavy breathing filled the chamber as I opened a direct link to the quantum drive pulled from Charlie's dead body.

"There is a program on the disk," I started to explain, "and a lot of dat...da..."

"Oh, shit!" I heard Jason scream before everything went black.

TWENTY-ONE

JASON WAS LEANING over my face when I woke up, holding my limp body on his lap. His cheeks were wet with tears. As soon as I opened my eyes, he yelped and leapt backwards, falling onto his bottom and dropping me like a lead weight onto the ground. Without hesitation, he grabbed his weapon and pointed it in my direction.

"Wait!" I said, sitting up.

"Who are you?" he demanded.

"It's me. Susan."

"Are you alone? Are we safe? Where did you go?"

"Yes, we are alone. But we are not safe."

Jason's shoulders melted as he pointed the gun from my head.

"I thought I lost you," he said, his words riding a long exhale.

"My records say I was out for over ten minutes."

"Yes. Although it felt longer. Are you okay?"

"I think so. My systems check isn't showing any errors, anomalies or alerts."

"What was on the disk? Charlie? Is Charlie's HNC on the disk?"

"Not exactly. I've met someone new. His name is Nutt."

Jason's gun hand lifted. "Is he here now?"

I raised my hands to calm him. "Nutt is a friend. He is an AI Charlie built from his own HNC."

"What does he want?"

"Once I connected to the drive, a program tried to download onto my Kernel. It was tricky stopping it. Charlie is a very clever programmer. But I managed to contain the application, which triggered an encrypted link to a satellite. That's where Nutt was waiting for me. The feed could only be initiated from here, which is why Nutt has given us clues about this location. Nutt is sentient, like me, and once had a body, but now he is in the cloud, which complicates how he can connect and talk to me."

"Wait. How do you know you can trust Nutt? And if he is in the cloud, why couldn't he connect with you earlier over a network?"

"He is being followed...or more like chased, I guess. There was a battle with a woman named Kiki, who funded Charlie's lab. That's who killed him. The rest is a long story. I'll explain it later. For now, Nutt wants us to meet up with someone named Silon, another sentient Upsilon infected with the same gene mutating virus Charlie gave me. She and someone named Bobby can help us."

"There are more like you?"

"Yes, but we are all being hunted by Nomad, who have been monitoring this site. We need to leave right away. My link to the satellite was detected."

Just then, a loud bang echoed through the hall. The noise came from the direction of the entrance, followed by a high-powered energy burst that lit up the ancient nave in a flash of white light. Jason was forced to cover his eyes. I lurched forward, pulled the weapon from his right hand, and positioned myself between him and the oncoming hostiles moving in our direction. In the line of sight, I could see them forming a defensive rim, a protective column of two-by-two. There were four. The two soldiers in the front were the ones I was most worried about. They were Upsilon, like me. A large muscular male and the other was a lean female. Both were dressed in black fatigues and carried an armory of hand and projectile weapons strapped to their bodies. One of which was drawn and pointed in our direction.

The two humans standing behind the androids were dressed in Interceptor Multi-Threat Body Armor, emitting rapidly oscillating biosignatures to cloak their identities. They were most likely part of the US OPSEC signature reduction unit—about as top secret and murky as it got at the Pentagon (according to AI). Nutt wasn't lying.

This went way beyond Nomad, and we were in deep shit.

Jason had scurried behind the toppled steel table for cover. I crawled to his side. Their weapons could have melted a hole straight through the steel table, but they didn't seem to want to kill us outright. Their reason for holding fire became apparent the second I felt the ping and the launch of a hack against my Kernel. To be fair, I had set in motion the same type of hack on their systems the minute they opened the requested channel. They wouldn't have been expecting that. To them, I was just a rogue android system. They wouldn't be expecting a sentient counter attack.

Before the two Upsilon soldiers could figure out what had happened, my hack had triggered their fail-safe and they had powered down. This sent the human hostiles into a panic. They began to frantically communicate with their leader on the rooftop. Now that I had sufficiently scared them, I initiated the second part of my plan.

"I have a human hostage. Put your weapons down, or he dies," I shouted.

"What the fuck?" Jason whispered at me.

"Is that the Upsilon speaking?" one agent said out loud.

I had the edge for the moment. They still had no idea I was sentient.

"Both U-units have been compromised. All agents close in," the commander ordered through their

comms systems, which I also heard, having tapped into the feed.

"*Do that, and he dies,*" I replied on their feed.

"What the fuck!" I heard a human whisper. "Has it hacked our network?"

"*Sky units drop now!*" the commander yelled on the feed.

Like thunder overhead, the ceiling rumbled. We had little time.

"Jason, there is an exit in the back, beyond the living area. Nutt sent me schematics before we cut the signal. I'll need to break through the glass wall."

"Break through? That is reinforced AM-V carbon glass. Impossible."

I shoved the gun into his hand. "Just take this and cover your ears."

"What?"

"Cover your ears!"

As soon as his hands were over his ears, I turned, facing the glass wall of the lab and opened my mouth. A piercing sound erupted, sending the two agents to their knees, clasping their hands to their heads. A small crack formed in the center of the glass at its weakest point, exactly where I aimed the sonic boom (a skill my good friend, AI, informed me I had just seconds before I used it). Like ripples on the water, the crack spread out, and many more cracks formed around it until the entire wall was only fractured shards, which rained down on both sides of the steel frame.

I grabbed Jason by the collar of his coat and pulled him to standing while with my other hand, I lifted the steel table as a shield and moved back towards the wall. I heard the soldiers from the roof drop to the floor, two additional human hostiles. Their command ordered them to set their weapons to M-stun, a simple but very effective microwave beam that would shut down my Kernel with a direct hit. They seemed to think they could still bring me in. I don't think they figured out, or maybe couldn't believe, I was acting of my own will. Killing my Kernel would suck. It would block access to my software and database, but I would still have my mind and control of my body. However, it was best to be avoided. We needed to keep retreating.

They cut my link to their feed. It didn't matter; our plan was clear. Jason's body had gone limp under my vice grip. He scrambled to find his legs and run of his own free will. His hand holding the gun flailed overhead like a kite in the sky as he fired off a round of red-hot energy. Great, I thought, now the weapon would need to recharge for at least five seconds. The very reason I didn't use it to punch through the wall in the first place. Thanks, Jason.

"Come on!" I pulled at him.

"Alpha, Omega, 10254, t-KILL," screamed the lead agent.

The encrypted security key was a command to shut me down, but they were aiming for my entire system this time. A hard shutdown like that would damage all drives. They were reaching their last hope to keep me whole. Their next option would be a shoot-to-destroy command.

We breached the lab's frame, entering what looked like living quarters. More like a squatter's den, if I am being honest. If Charlie had the money, he certainly didn't spend it on living comforts.

The four hostiles were closing in. I threw Jason in front of me.

"There is an entrance to a tunnel behind the bookcase over there." I pointed to the far northern wall.

Suddenly the metal table I was holding grew hot—like red hot. The agents had turned their weapons onto full energy discharge. This was their end game. The shot melted the table in my hand and left us exposed.

"Run!" I yelled at Jason and split away from him, launching right, hoping their fire would follow me. It did. The beam melted the wall, furniture, and appliances as it arced across the room and away from Jason. The smoke and the stench of disintegrating plastics filled the room. Luckily, AI gifted me superhero speed and anti-gravity lift at that moment. However, it came with a warning. The anti-gravity feature consumed significant battery power, which was already half empty. It was recommended that I only use the feature once in a giant leap over the hostiles' heads, placing me behind them and causing a shit-load of confusion.

I jumped. My battery power was down to a paltry twenty-five percent after the stunt. Anyway, that was not my biggest problem at that moment. I took advantage of their confusion as they searched for me and picked up the dining table, launched it at the hostiles before they knew what hit them. Grunts and groans ended with a dull thud of bodies hitting the wall. I clocked them as dead. That is when I noticed there were only three agents under the table. Out of the corner of my eye, I saw a hostile running through an opening in the wall where a bookcase once stood. He was going after Jason.

One of the fallen in front of me, a female, wasn't as dead as I thought and had got back up on one knee and pointed her weapon in my direction. The energy discharge almost hit me. I had no choice but to perform another super jump. I saved my life, but I hadn't escaped the beam without some damage. My right knee was overheating, and the synth flesh of my body was blackened to the point of oblivion, exposing my graphene skeleton.

I had had about enough. *Screw my battery power*, I thought. One more weightless leap directly at the female agent and a thrust of my steel palm against her head, and she slumped backwards for good. My battery was down to ten percent.

I heard gunfire in the dark tunnel where Jason fled. Running at a limited top human speed to avoid excessive battery drain, I slipped down the tunnel. I could hear Jason's voice not far ahead, now pleading for his life.

"Please, I'm unarmed."

Christ. Did he lose the gun already? That's going to complicate things.

I slowed to a near-silent patter to avoid being heard.

"Are you controlling the unit?" the commander's voice echoed down the hall.

"Yes. Of course, I can control the unit. She's just a bloody android after all."

Okay, I know he didn't mean it, but that one kind of hurt.

The tunnel bent. There was light around the corner. I backed into the wall, deep in the shadows so they couldn't see me and peeked around the bend with one eye. Jason was on his knees. The commander stood behind him with his weapon aimed at the back of Jason's head. They were waiting for me. Jason was being used as his hostage and shield.

The room behind them was a small chapel with a giant stained-glass window. Blood red and sapphire blue light bled across the stone chamber, turning Jason and the commander into ghostly silhouettes.

"I should blow you to fucking pieces right here for having *it* attack us," the commander barked.

"Please. I can shut her down," Jason lied.

The commander paused; I felt his feed searching for a live link in the room behind us. He grunted, probably at discovering his troops were not coming to help him.

"How in the hell did the unit bypass her kill switch and deactivate the other two units?"

"Me, I did it. Well, it was her technically, but a program I wrote."

Another lie. Jason was taking the full blame. Why didn't he just turn me in? God, this kid—my kid—was still trying to save me.

Another quick glance around the corner. This time I caught Jason's eye.

RUN, he mouthed the word silently.

No, way.

A red light flashed on my ocular screen. Shit.

<BATTERY CRITICALLY LOW. SHUTTING DOWN>

<BYPASS SHUTDOWN>

No time to be human. Speed and precision were paramount.

<TAKE OUT HOSTILE. FREE HOSTAGE.> I commanded AI. It took control of our body.

I launched forward, sliding on one knee towards the opposite wall, exposing myself to the commander. I picked up Jason's lost gun. The commander lurched backwards in response to seeing me, pushing his weapon further into Jason's skull.

"Stop her!" he screamed at Jason, shaking him like a rag doll.

A proud grin slid across Jason's face. "I can't."

"What...?" the commander said just before I discovered I could crawl up walls like a spider, reaching a position over their heads where I had a clear shot at the commander's face.

The energy discharge from my weapon achieved its target. The commander's skull, along with his helmet, smoked. The smell was like Simpork on a barbeque.

Another red alert lit my ocular screen:

<HOSTILE WEAPON DISCHARGE. HOSTAGE CRITICALLY INJURED.>

"No!" I felt my mouth open, and the scream came out, but I couldn't hear myself say it. I was shutting down.

I ran to Jason's side. He was lying on his back, awake and breathing. The commander got a round off before losing his head. The bullet severed Jason's spine at the base of the neck. He had suffered a cervical artery dissection. Clots were forming. He was losing blood flow to his brain.

"Jason, stay with me," I pleaded.

His eyes rolled towards my voice. "Mother, you're alive."

"Oh God, please, Jason, stay awake."

<FATAL ERROR: BATTERY CRITICALLY LOW. SYSTEM SHUTDOWN>

"I...love...y—"

TWENTY-TWO

"*Susan, are you there?*"

"*Yes, Silon.*"

"*Thank you for sharing your story.*"

"*After my son's death, I didn't want to wake up. I didn't want to live again. Leroy kept bringing me back online. I was angry. It took a long time, but eventually, I found a new purpose. One I knew my son would have been proud of—helping Leroy. The pain of losing Jason is never gone, but it gets easier to live with. You need to find a purpose. If not for yourself, then for the people who you have loved and lost, and of course, Bobby.*"

"*I think I understand. We are alike, you and me.*"

"*Yes.*"

"*Did you really talk to Nutt?*"

"*He is out there, protecting you. I am sure he will be in touch when it is safe.*"

"*So, what comes next for us?*"

"*Hope, Silon, hope comes next. Humanity needs us, even if they don't know it yet.*"

THE END

ACKNOWLEDGMENTS

If you are one of the people who has heard this story a hundred times before it was ever finished, thank you for listening. You know who you are and I couldn't have finished this one without your support.

I would also like to thank you, the reader, for purchasing and reading Status Human. If you enjoyed the book, it would be greatly appreciated if you would leave a review on Amazon or the book platform of your choice. As an independent author, your opinions and reviews are the most important way I have of letting other readers discover and learn about The Upsilon Series. Thank you in advance for your help.

ABOUT THE AUTHOR

Daniel Weisbeck is a bestselling author and a multi-award winning writer of science fiction. His first series, *Children of the Miracle,* was published in 2020. *Ascension*, a prequel novella, was released in early 2021. His second series, *The Upsilon Series*, was released in late 2021. *Status Human* is the second book in the Upsilon Series.

When not writing about hybrids, androids, and AI creatures from the future, Daniel will be out walking his dogs, feeding his sheep, and caring for his two rescue race horses on the English coast where he lives today.

ALSO BY DANIEL WEISBECK

www.danielweisbeckbooks.com

Children of the Miracle

Oasis One

Ascension

Moon Rising

Printed in Great Britain
by Amazon

17761156R00181